the
last
wild
place

the last wild place

ROSA JORDAN

PEACHTREE
ATLANTA

Published by
PEACHTREE PUBLISHERS
1700 Chattahoochee Avenue
Atlanta, Georgia 30318-2112

www.peachtree-online.com

Text © 2008 by Rosa Jordan

Cover design by Loraine M. Joyner
Book design by Melanie McMahon Ives

Manufactured in the United States of America
10 9 8 7 6 5 4 3 2 1
First Edition

Library of Congress Cataloging-in-Publication Data

Jordan, Rosa.
  The last wild place / by Rosa Jordan. -- 1st ed.
    p. cm.
  Summary: With problems mounting at home and with his best friend, when sixth-grader Chip discovers a family of Florida panthers in the marshy woods behind an abandoned farm, he puts aside his own predicaments and concentrates on finding a safe home for the wild animals.
  ISBN 978-1-56145-458-7
  [1. Endangered species--Fiction. 2. Florida panther--Fiction. 3. Puma--Fiction. 4. Friendship--Fiction. 5. Florida--Fiction.] I. Title.
  PZ7.J76815Las 2008
  [Fic]--dc22
                                        2008008785

For Vicky Holifield, my editor,
whose magic touch always makes a good story better

Contents

1
Welcome Home

Chip awoke to a loud thump. Something big was moving around in his bedroom. He squinted into the dark, waiting for his eyes to adjust, then heard another thump and felt his bed shake.

"Junk all over the place!" the intruder muttered. "Coulda killed myself."

Chip sat up. There, standing in the moonlight flooding in through the bedroom window, was his brother Justin—or else he was having a very vivid dream.

"Justin? What are you doing here?"

"Trying to find my bed. Which appears to be buried under *your* crap." Clothes, comic books, a baseball glove, and video games went sailing through the air as Justin flung Chip's stuff off his bed.

Chip switched on the bedside lamp. "I mean, what are you doing home? Did you get kicked out of college already?"

"Course not! Booker was coming down to visit his family, and he asked if I wanted to come along."

Booker Wilson was one of Chip's favorite people. Even though he lost his lower legs in the Gulf War, he was still just about the best pitcher Chip knew of. And Booker was everybody's friend, even if they'd just known him for five minutes.

He'd grown up at the other end of Lost Goat Lane, but now he coached baseball at the college Justin went to in Atlanta. If it hadn't been for Booker, Justin would have dropped out of baseball back in ninth grade. But he listened to Booker, and it was a good thing too, because he ended up with an athletic scholarship.

Chip was about to ask Justin more questions, but just then he heard voices coming from the kitchen. "Who's that?" he asked.

"Mom."

"But who's she talking to?"

"Booker."

"Booker's here?" Chip yelped. "I gotta go say hi!"

"You stay put," Justin said. "We're only going to be here two days. This is probably the one chance they'll have to be alone."

Why would they want to be alone? Chip wondered as headed down the hall. When he reached the darkened living room he could see the brightly lit kitchen and the back of Booker's wheelchair. But just as he was about to say hello, something stopped him in his tracks.

Mom was sitting on Booker's lap.

She was holding a bunch of red roses, and she was laughing. "Booker Wilson, you are too much!" Chip heard her say. "I can't believe you drove four hundred miles just to bring me flowers! At my age!"

"What age?" Booker said. "You keeping score or something?"

Just then a hand clamped on Chip's shoulder and dragged him backward. The hand belonged to his sixteen-year-old sister Kate. "Don't be spying on them!" she hissed. Then she moved in front of Chip so *she* could spy on them.

"Oh my gosh!" she gasped.

2

"What?" Chip whispered. "Let me see." He pushed her to one side so he could look into the kitchen again. What he saw made his mouth drop open. Mom and Booker were *kissing*.

Kate grabbed him by the hand and dragged him down the hall to his room. Justin was sprawled on his bed. Kate flipped on the light and closed the bedroom door behind her. "Justin!" she whispered. "*What* is going on?"

Chip climbed back into bed and waited for Justin's explanation. All Justin said was, "You could say hello."

"Hel-lo," Kate said in an exaggerated voice and sat down on the edge of Chip's bed. "Now tell me what's going on!"

"I give up," Justin yawned. "What's going on?"

"Mom and Booker! I thought he *had* a girlfriend."

"Melody? Nah. She's history."

"You mean they broke up?" Kate demanded.

"Yeah. About a year ago. Booker said she got a job in D.C. after she finished law school. He heard she's engaged to a congressman."

"Oh." Kate sat there a minute, then asked, "So when did this thing with Mom and Booker come about?"

"What thing?"

"They're out there like...like they're on a date or something!" Kate stuck her fingers in her blonde hair and grabbed hold of her scalp like the idea was about to cause her head to explode.

"They're *kissing!*" Chip informed his brother.

"So? No law against that."

"Justin!" Kate leaned across Chip, half squishing him, and whacked Justin on the arm. "Stop acting so superior! This is *serious*."

"Serious how?" asked Justin. "They've been friends since before we were born."

3

"I know that!" Kate snapped. "But since when did they get to be a couple?"

"I don't see why you're so upset," Justin said.

"I'm not upset." Kate took a deep breath. "I'm just saying that it would be…I don't know…hard for them to be a couple. I mean—"

"You mean because Booker's black?" Justin asked.

"Booker's not black," Chip interrupted. "He's very dark brown. Same as Luther and Ruby and the rest of the Wilsons."

"And Luther is Chip's best friend and Ruby's your best friend," Justin said to Kate. "You saying it's *not* okay for Mom and Booker to go out together?"

"No! I mean, yes! Of course it's okay. I'm just saying…some of my friends might not understand."

Chip could see why his sister was confused. They had barely known the Wilsons until four years ago, when Kate's nanny goat ran away to visit the Wilsons' billy goat. First it was the goats that got acquainted, but that same day Chip and Luther got to be buddies. Later, Kate and Ruby started making gourmet chocolates to sell, and then they started a home sewing business together called Denim Designs. Now Kate and Ruby were together practically every weekend, either at home making stuff or in town selling it. Kate did have a few friends her own age now, but back in junior high she'd gotten a lot of hassle about her unstylish clothes and farm-girl image. If word about Booker and Mom got around, Kate might start getting teased all over again.

They stopped talking when they heard the kitchen door open and close, then the thump of Booker's wheelchair being let down the steps to the ground. Voices coming from outside told them that Mom was walking Booker to his van.

"Besides," Kate said, no longer whispering, "Mom's a lot older than Booker. Four years older, at least."

"Yeah, and she's divorced and has three kids. On top of that, Booker's in a wheelchair, and his skin's darker than ours," Justin said. "Booker and me had a long talk about it on the drive down from Atlanta. Looks to me like none of that stuff's a problem for him. If Mom gave him a welcome-home kiss, I guess it's not a problem for her either. If it's a problem for you, Kate, well, that's your problem." Justin rolled over to face the wall. "Turn off the light, Chip, so I can get some sleep."

Kate stood up to leave. "It's not a problem for *you* because you're off in college now and don't have to live in this little town, where nobody ever saw a mixed-race couple except on TV!"

"So," Justin yawned, "tell 'em Booker's a TV star and Mom's gonna be his leading lady."

Chip turned off the light. Kate stalked out and slammed the door so hard Chip wondered if Mom might have heard it out in the yard. Booker's van drove away, but Chip could tell Mom was still on the front porch. He could hear the squeak of the swing as it moved back and forth. She was singing softly. She had a good voice. She probably really could have been on TV if she'd wanted to be a singer.

He reckoned his friends wouldn't give him any flack about Mom and Booker. They'd each just wish Booker was stuck on *their* mom so he'd hang around their house and play baseball with *them*.

"Justin," he said to his brother's back. "I think this might be a win-win-win situation."

"That's the way I look at it," his brother murmured, half asleep.

2
Bad Day for Luther

Justin and Kate were still asleep when Chip got up the next morning, and Mom had already gone to work at Mr. Hashimoto's plant nursery just across the highway.

Chip poured himself a bowl of cereal and read the note Mom had left on the table.

Chip, be sure to change into clean clothes before going to town. Kate, when you and Ruby finish your candy making, please put the roast in the oven. Justin, will you replace the overhead light on the back porch? If you go off with your friends, don't forget to leave a phone number where you'll be.

Mom

Ever since Dad had left, which was almost before Chip could remember, Mom had worked full time, so she had to do a lot of parenting-by-note. In a way it wasn't bad, because it meant she wasn't around to nag them about little stuff. But if she got home and you hadn't finished all the jobs on the list, look out!

After breakfast Chip did his regular chores—milking the goats and feeding the ducks. He strained the milk and put it in the fridge, then headed down Lost Goat Lane toward the

Wilson house. He looked for turtles in the drainage ditch that ran alongside the unpaved road, but all he saw was one snapping turtle. He didn't try to catch it, as he once would have, but he watched it awhile. This year he had learned in Mr. O'Dell's biology class that if you just observe things without disturbing them, you can see critters do whatever they would be doing if they weren't being watched. When the turtle disappeared under the water, Chip walked on.

Up ahead was the Wilson farm, which was pretty much the same as Chip's family's, with a shade tree in the front yard and a goat pen and pasture out back. Booker's van was parked in front of the house. Chip hadn't exactly forgotten about Mom and Booker, but right now he had other things to think about. He and Luther had a big day ahead of them.

Chip was about to knock on the front door when he heard yelling. He was so surprised that his hand stopped in midair and just hung there, fingers still curled to make knuckles for knocking. Old Mr. and Mrs. Wilson, usually soft-spoken, only yelled when they were calling to somebody outside. Booker had a booming voice, but Chip had never seen him mad enough to yell like this. He'd heard Ruby raise her voice plenty of times, but what he heard coming from the kitchen weren't her high-pitched yells. It was definitely Luther, normally the quietest person in the whole family, who was making most of the noise.

"No!" Luther shouted. "I'm staying here!"

Then several voices spoke all at once. Chip couldn't make out what they were saying, only that they seemed to be trying to calm Luther down. Then Luther yelled again, "You can't make me! If you try, I'll run away from home!" With that, the back door slammed so hard that Chip could feel the vibration all the way to the front porch.

Chip was turning to go after him and find out why he was so mad when a voice behind him said, "Oh, hi, Chip." Luther's mother Ruby opened the screen door and came out onto the porch.

"I just got here," Chip blurted out, hoping she wouldn't think he'd been on the porch for half an hour listening to their family fight. He glanced at her, then looked away quickly. Chip had never seen her this upset. She wasn't actually crying, but her eyes were wet. Even all teared up like that she was about the prettiest woman Chip knew. "Um...I..." he stammered. "I was looking for—"

"Luther's out back," Ruby said before he could finish.

"He probably went to get Old Billy," Chip said, trying to sound cheerful. "We're going to give him a bath before we take him to town."

"Oh, that's right." Ruby took a deep breath and added, "Tell Luther I'll be at your house, helping Kate make candy. You boys want to stop by on your way to town, I'll save you a piece."

"Thanks!" Chip never missed a chance for a sample of the hand-dipped chocolates Ruby and Kate made. He took off around the corner of the house. Luther was coming from the pasture, leading Old Billy.

Old Billy was not your average goat. He was pure white with long, beautiful horns that curved out toward the ends. Over the years, he'd won tons of prizes at county and state fairs. People brought their nannies from all over to breed with him in hopes of getting baby goats of the same good quality. Two of the Martins' milk goats, Honey and Go-Girl, were Old Billy's offspring, but they weren't snowy white like him. Little Billy, the third of the triplets and the one who looked most like Old Billy, was now a mascot for the marching band at Justin's college.

Chip watched as Luther led Old Billy across the pasture. He had to admit that the old goat still had style. Old Billy practically pranced when he walked.

Luther, though, was not prancing. He was scuffing his feet through the grass, looking miserable.

Chip opened the gate so Luther could lead Billy into the yard. "Hey, man. What's happening?"

"Crap's happening, that's what," Luther grumbled. "Get the hose, will you?"

Chip went to the spigot and turned it on. Then he uncoiled the garden hose and carried it to where Luther was holding Billy.

"Good morning, Chip," Mrs. Wilson called from the porch. "Here's some herbal shampoo you can use. I reckon the children will appreciate Old Billy more if he smells nice."

Luther turned his back and didn't answer, so Chip went to get the shampoo. When Mrs. Wilson handed him the bottle, she looked past him, out to where Luther was starting to hose down Old Billy. She watched Luther with worried eyes for a minute, then went back into the house.

One thing about being a person's best friend for four years, you know when to keep quiet. Chip could tell Luther was not in the mood to talk, so he didn't ask him what was wrong. Old Billy smelled pretty rank, so Chip poured a thick line of green shampoo along his backbone, from between his horns all the way to his tail. He started working it into a lather all over one side of Billy's body. Luther dropped the hose and started lathering the other side. Pretty soon Billy looked like one giant mound of soapsuds.

Luther flicked some suds off Billy's spine onto Chip. Naturally Chip flicked some back at him. In a minute they were throwing handfuls of suds at each other. By the time Mr. Wilson

9

came out to see how they were getting along, they were as covered in suds as Old Billy, and laughing like fools.

"You boys line up with Billy and I'll hose all of you off together," Mr. Wilson said with a chuckle.

"I'll do it," Luther said, picking up the hose. He doused himself, then turned the spray on Chip.

"Hey, that's enough!" Chip protested. "Old Billy's the one who needs the bath!"

Mr. Wilson handed Chip a small container. "Here's the polish for his horns and hooves, but make sure he's good and dry before you apply it."

"Yes sir," Chip said. When he looked up, Booker was coming across the yard in his wheelchair.

"Hey, men," Booker boomed. "I thought Old Billy only got the royal treatment for Fall Fair. What's the occasion? He got a lady friend coming to visit?"

"Not today," Mr. Wilson answered as he fed Billy a biscuit left over from breakfast. "Him and these boys are heading to town to be good citizens, helping out some folks that fell on hard times."

"What folks are we talking about?" Booker wanted to know.

"Them people along the Gulf Coast that got blown this way by that last hurricane," Mr. Wilson explained. "There's a fair number still living in the community center, families whose homes were completely wiped out."

"I see how the boys might be some help, but where does Old Billy fit in?" Booker asked. "Goats aren't especially known as good citizens."

"Some of the families staying at the center have kids," Mr. Wilson explained. "And not all that much for them to do. Chip and Luther came up with the idea of going over and giving them free rides in the goat cart."

"What an amazingly good idea!" Booker gave Chip and Luther one of his superwide grins, the kind that make you feel warm from the inside out. "I mean, brilliant! One of you guys decide to be president when you grow up, you got my vote!"

"Thanks," Chip said, pleased to be doing something Booker thought was a good idea. He cut a sidelong look at Luther. Luther hadn't said anything, but he was wearing a little smile. Chip could tell that his anger was wearing off.

When the grown-ups went back in the house, Chip and Luther rubbed Billy down, then flopped down in the grass to wait for him to get dry. It was a perfect spring day, the kind where the sun is warm enough to make you feel lazy, but not so hot that it turns you into a puddle of sweat.

"Bet you're glad Booker's home," Chip said. He was considering whether or not to tell Luther about Mom and Booker. He and Luther didn't keep secrets from each other—ever. Chip just wasn't sure about the kissing part. What if Luther laughed and started cracking jokes about it, the way Chip knew his other friends would do if they found out?

Luther didn't answer, so Chip decided to wait a while before bringing up the subject. Instead he said, "This is going to be a fun day."

"This is *not* a fun day," Luther snapped. "It's the second-worst day of my life."

Chip sat up and stared at him. "Why?"

"Because my mother is getting married, that's why." Luther picked up a pebble and threw it as hard as he could at the side of the house. Fortunately it struck below the window. Chip wasn't sure whether Luther had been aiming at the window or not.

"To Mr. Jackson?" Richard Jackson was a math teacher at the local high school. Ruby had been going out with him for more than three years, so the fact that they'd finally decided to get married wasn't any big surprise. And as far as Chip knew, Luther liked him okay. "You reckon that's going to be a problem?"

"The problem," Luther snarled, "is that when they get married, my mom plans to move in with him. Which means *I'll* have to move."

"Oh." That, Chip had to admit, would be a problem, not just for Luther, but for him too. A lot of the things they did together wouldn't be so easy if Luther lived in town. On the other hand, it wouldn't be all that bad to have a place in town to hang out.

"Well, his apartment's close to the junior high," Chip reminded him. "If you go out for the baseball team next year, it would be easier if you didn't have to take the bus. And," he added cheerfully, "Mr. Jackson can help you with your math. If we get Terrible Thackery for seventh-grade math, we're going to need all the help we can get."

"You think I want to spend all day in school, then go home to an apartment that's right next to the school to live with a teacher and do more schoolwork? I'd rather *flunk* math!" Luther picked up another, bigger rock and flung it. Chip winced when it thwacked against the side of the house. Right now Luther probably wouldn't have cared if the rock had hit the glass and shattered it all over the floor of his mother's bedroom.

"You got a point," Chip said. "But breaking a window probably won't help the situation."

Luther took off his soapsuds-spattered glasses and started polishing them on the tail of his T-shirt. "Nothing's going to help the situation," he muttered.

The cheerfulness Chip had felt when he was walking down Lost Goat Lane on the way to the Wilson farm, looking forward to their trip to town, had worn off. Luther's situation, he was just figuring out, might actually be *their* situation.

Luther was worried about having to move into town if his mom got married. Well, what if Chip's mom decided to marry Booker? Would she want to move to Atlanta? That wouldn't matter to Justin, since he was already living there. And it wouldn't affect Kate so much. In one more year she'd graduate and go off to college. But what about Chip? And what about their goats? Suddenly Chip felt sick. Luther looked like he didn't feel so hot either. Neither of them said anything for a long time.

Then a question crossed Chip's mind. "You said this was the second-worst day of your life, Luther. What's the worst?"

"The worst," Luther said darkly, "will be the day they get married and Mama tries to make me move to town with her and Mr. Jackson. Because I won't do it. I already told her, I'll run away first."

3
Good Citizens

As soon as they got Old Billy brushed and polished, they headed up Lost Goat Lane to Chip's house so he could change clothes. Chip asked Luther if he wanted to come in, but Luther scowled and said he would wait outside with Old Billy.

Chip put on a clean T-shirt and shorts, then went into the kitchen where Kate and Luther's mom Ruby were making candy. Kate was looking out the window at Luther and Old Billy. "Why didn't you bring the cart?"

"Mr. Wilson didn't want us to take theirs," Chip explained. "He said it's too big. Two or three kids might pile in, and Old Billy not being as young as he used to be, it would be too heavy for him. He said it'd be better to take Lily's cart."

The brightly painted cart Chip was referring to wasn't really Lily Hashimoto's, it was her father's. Mr. Hashimoto used it at the nursery to display potted plants. It was a lot smaller than the Wilsons' cart, barely big enough for one small child to perch on its seat.

Chip wandered over to the kitchen counter and looked at the candy laid out on wax paper. He hoped Ruby hadn't forgotten her promise to give him a piece.

"It's nearly noon," Ruby said. "Wouldn't you boys like some lunch before you leave?"

"They're having a hot dog roast at the center. We'll eat there." Chip cast one more longing look at the candy and turned to go.

But Ruby did remember. "Go ahead, have one." She smiled. "And take one for Luther too."

Chip ate his piece of candy on the way out the door. When he offered Luther the other one, he shook his head. Chip almost popped it in his own mouth, but he held onto it until they got across the highway. Just before reaching the nursery, he offered the chocolate to him again. This time, too far away for his mother to see, Luther ate it.

Lily was in the nursery parking lot kicking a soccer ball around. Her father had forbidden soccer practice in the parking lot because he was afraid she might ding a customer's car. But when there were only a few cars in the lot, like this morning, she did it anyway. She said her soccer kicks were so accurate that if she ever put a ding in somebody's car, it would be on purpose.

As they walked toward her, Chip thought that was probably true. It was amazing that a girl so small was the best soccer player in the whole elementary school.

When Lily saw them coming she grabbed the shanks of the cart and pulled it into the middle of the parking lot. Mr. Hashimoto would freak out if he saw a goat anywhere near his plants. Lily had removed the potted plants from the cart and had given it a good scrubbing. Old Billy seemed to know it was done for his benefit, because he headed straight for it.

Luther and Lily got into a squabble over who should put Billy's harness on him. When Lily insisted, Luther stood back and waited until she got all the lines tangled up. Finally Lily had to ask for help. Luther politely took the harness, like he'd tried to do in the first place, and had it untangled in two minutes. Chip backed Old Billy in between the shafts, and the boys fastened the buckles on each side. It was quick and easy for them; they'd done it hundreds of times in the four years since they'd first trained Old Billy to pull a cart. As they started off, Lily flipped the soccer ball into the cart.

"What are you taking that along for?" asked Luther.

"Only the littlest kids can ride in this cart," Lily pointed out. "I'll organize a soccer game for the others."

"Good idea," Chip said.

The road to town used to go past farms and sugarcane fields, but now it was lined with businesses; some new housing tracts had been built farther back. The path they followed along the highway used to be shady almost all the way. Now most of the Australian pines had been cut down to make room for driveways and parking lots.

It took half an hour to walk to the community center. A lot of grown-ups—mostly women—were sitting in folding chairs on the shady side of the building, talking like they might do on their porch at home, if they had a home anymore. Some held babies in their laps, and others watched the toddlers playing nearby.

A little distance away, some people from town were setting up long tables and piling food on them. Kids were running all over the place, not doing anything in particular, just acting kind of wild the way kids did at school when the playground monitor wasn't paying attention. As soon as the children saw the goat cart, though, they rushed over and surrounded it, pushing and shoving to get up close. Old Billy snorted, which meant he was annoyed. Chip and Luther tried to get the kids to back up and give him some space, but some of the bigger boys weren't listening.

Lily put two fingers in her mouth and let out a whistle that probably dented every eardrum for a block around. She lifted the soccer ball out of the cart, held it over her head, and announced: "The cart is for *little* kids. Soccer's for anybody who's old enough." Then she walked off toward the other side of the field. A few of the big kids hung around for a few minutes, peering into the cart or trying to pet Old Billy, but when their curiosity was satisfied, they ran to catch up with Lily.

When Chip turned around, he found a small girl, maybe three years old, with her arms wrapped around Billy's neck. She was crying, and he didn't know what to do. Finally her mother came over and explained that they used to have a white goat that looked a lot like Old Billy.

"After the hurricane we took Snowball up on the roof with us," the sad-eyed mother explained. "But when the helicopter came to rescue us, it wouldn't take the goat, and Saralee's been crying ever since. She's just too little to understand about things like that."

"She can have the first ride," Luther said. The young mother thanked him and put Saralee in the cart. Luther led Old Billy in a long loop around the community center grounds. By the time the cart got back, Chip had nine other preschoolers lined up to take turns.

All of the little kids got a ride in the cart except for one toddler who fell down and skinned his knees and had to be carried off by his mom to get cleaned up. Chip was just about to ask Luther if they should give the kids a second ride when he heard a scream.

Chip swung around and looked toward the soccer field. Lily was down. A big boy loomed over her, looking like he'd rather kick her than the soccer ball. Chip had seen the boy at school. His name was Ruben, and even though he looked much older, he was only in fifth grade.

Chip raced toward the field, Luther alongside him. They both knew that Lily's piercing scream didn't mean she was hurt. It meant she was mad. They didn't need to save Lily. They needed to save the boy. She was going to come up off the ground any moment now, and what happened next would not be pretty.

Of course, Ruben, being a newcomer, couldn't have known that. When Chip and Luther ran up, he turned to confront them. "She kept fouling me!" he shouted. "She's a dirty little cheater!"

Luther dealt with Ruben while Chip helped Lily to her feet, staying between her and Ruben to be sure she didn't try to punch him in the stomach. It was all Chip could do to hold her back.

"Take it easy!" Luther urged Ruben. "It's not a real game. She'd get called if it was."

"Would not!" Lily yelled. "Every time I beat him to the ball he fell all over me! He fouled *me!*"

Chip could hold Lily back, but he couldn't shut her up. And if she didn't shut up, there was a good chance that all three of them were going to get seriously smacked around by Ruben and his friends.

Then a scream even louder than Lily's echoed across the field. The kids forgot the fight and turned to stare.

A large gray-haired black woman and an even larger red-headed white woman were crossing to the tables carrying an ice chest between them. One was yelling: *"You nasty goat! Get away from that table!"*

What Chip saw next made his hair stand on end. Old Billy was over by the picnic table with a bag of hot dog buns dangling from his mouth. Chip fairly flew across the grass, Lily and Luther at his heels.

The two women had dropped the ice chest and were also heading for Old Billy. Fortunately, Chip, Luther, and Lily got there first. By then Billy had scattered the contents of one bag of buns on the ground and was about to rip open another one. Luther jerked it out of the goat's mouth, but it tore, scattering buns every which way. Billy snatched up one bun in his teeth and was standing there chomping on it when the two women came huffing up.

"Look at that!" shouted the big red-haired woman, whose face was so flushed she looked like she had a bad sunburn. "The food that goat has ruined!"

Billy stopped chewing and glowered at the women. The end of the hot dog bun stuck out of his mouth like a fat cigar.

"They're not all ruined!" Luther scooped up the buns from the grass and dumped them on the table. "These are okay. See? The grass is clean."

"He only tasted the one," Lily said. "I don't think he cares much for white bread."

"I'll eat this one," Chip said, snatching the bun out of the goat's mouth. He stuffed the remains of the bun into his pocket.

The gray-haired black woman put her hands on her hips and said, "You kids see that grill over there? Well, let me give you fair warning. If that goat is anywhere near this food table one minute from now, we're going to forget about hot dogs. We'll be serving folks barbecued goat!"

Luther took Billy's lead rope and dragged him toward the street. Chip gave the goat a push to hurry him along. Lily veered off to the soccer field. "Gotta get my soccer ball," she said.

"Oh no," Luther muttered. "She's going to get us killed."

"Hey, look!" Chip shouted. It was Booker's van pulling up to the curb.

Justin got out, carrying a softball and bat. It took Booker a few minutes to get out of the van and come around to where Chip, Luther, and Lily were. As usual, he was wearing the biggest smile this side of Santa Claus.

"How'd the goat cart rides go over?" Booker asked.

"Great," Luther answered. "The little kids loved them."

"How about the soccer game?" Justin asked, looking at Lily.

"They're jerks," Lily snapped. "Mean as snakes."

Booker looked from Lily to Chip to Luther. "That so?"

"Well," Luther said uncomfortably. "They are pretty tough. I know some of them from school and, well, they sort of run in a gang, all the community center kids."

"Not much point in trying to get along," Chip added. "Considering they're only here temporarily, till they get relocated."

"No point in them trying to get along with you, or you trying to get along with them?" Booker asked in the soft voice he used when he wanted you to think seriously about something.

"I was *trying* to be nice to them!" Lily complained. "All I got was pushed down and called a cheater, when it was *them* that kept fouling *me.*"

Chip knew without having watched the game that Lily was telling the truth, because he'd played soccer with her enough to know her style. She was super fast and very small, and she could get in right next to the ball in a way that caused other players to fall over her. Her opponents always got the foul called on them. It *was* frustrating.

Lily was halfway across the field. "You going back to play some more?" Justin called.

"No," she shouted without bothering to look back. "I'm going to get *my* soccer ball."

"How about sticking around for some softball?" Booker yelled. "Or is soccer the only sport you play?"

Lily stopped and turned around. "No, Booker," she said with a big grin. "Soccer's just my *best* sport."

"What about you two?" Justin asked Chip and Luther. "Ready for a game of work-up?"

Luther shook his head. "Old Billy's in a bad mood. We'd better get him home."

"Yeah," Chip said. "See you later."

Actually Chip would have loved to stay and play ball. For one thing, Booker was a fantastic ballplayer. But even more important, he was great at straightening things out between people. Life would be a lot easier for Chip at school if he could get on friendly terms with those big boys than it would if he left with them still mad and wanting to kick his butt.

But Luther was his best friend, and you don't ditch your best friend, not even for a chance to play ball with Booker Wilson and your big brother home from college.

4
Decisions

O ld Billy seemed tired after all the cart rides—either that or he was sulking because he hadn't been allowed to eat more of the hot dog buns. The goat plodded along slowly, so Chip and Luther didn't have to trot to keep up with him the way they usually did. They stopped at the nursery to unhook the cart and thank Mr. Hashimoto for letting them borrow it, then led Old Billy across the highway and turned down Lost Goat Lane.

It was past noon and Chip was hungry. "Want to stop at my house for lunch?" he asked, knowing already that Luther would say no because Ruby was still there, working with Kate to get their chocolate orders finished.

Luther shook his head. "I'd rather have what Grandma fixes. Let's get something at my house."

Chip nodded, and walked on past his house toward Luther's. He knew Luther was particular about what he ate. The first day they met, when they were only seven years old, Chip learned that Luther was a vegetarian. Luther had eaten a peanut butter sandwich instead of ham like everybody else. Chip had asked him if he didn't like ham, and Luther had said yes, he did like ham, but he liked pigs better. Chip was a sometimes-vegetarian himself, but if the meat was something he really liked, he ate it even though he also really liked animals. Hungry as he was right now, if the gnawed-on bun in his pocket had a hot dog in it he would have gladly eaten it, goat slobber and all.

When they reached the Wilson farm, they took Billy around back to feed him before going into the house to feed themselves. Mr. Wilson stuck his head out the back door. "Well, boys," he called, "how'd the goat cart rides go?"

"Great," Luther said.

"It was a good idea to just give rides to preschoolers," Chip added.

"I'm glad Billy behaved himself." Mr. Wilson beamed at his prize goat.

"I didn't say *that*," Luther corrected him. "He got us kicked off the community center grounds."

"Oh?" Mr. Wilson scratched his curly white hair. "How'd that come about?"

As they described how they had let go of Billy to help Lily and how Billy had helped himself to a few packages of hot dog buns, Mr. Wilson began to chuckle. Chip had to admit that now that it was over, it was pretty funny.

They fed Billy, wiped him down the way they'd been taught to do after he'd had a workout with the cart, then went into the kitchen. Mr. Wilson was already there, telling his wife what had happened.

Chip and Luther slid into chairs at the kitchen table, and Mrs. Wilson poured them each a glass of lemonade. "Those women!" She shook her head and laughed. "That would've been Mrs. Sikes and Mrs. Mosley. Sam, can't you just see those big ladies galloping across the lawn after that goat?"

That caused Mr. Wilson to explode into laughter. "Good thing you got to Billy before those ladies did! I don't know

Mrs. Sikes all that well, but Mrs. Mosley has a barbecue stand over on Lake Road. If you hadn't gotten Old Billy out of there, she'd have him on the menu by now."

Chip shot Luther a look and they both laughed.

"With all the uproar, did you boys get any lunch?" Mrs. Wilson asked.

"No," Luther said. "And I'm starving."

"Me too," Chip echoed.

Mrs. Wilson started taking stuff out of the fridge to make the kind of sandwiches that only she could—thick slices of home-baked bread filled with peanut butter and strawberry jam for Luther, rich, salty ham for Chip. Mrs. Wilson respected Luther's decision to be a vegetarian. She didn't mind fixing food for him that didn't have meat in it. And she always seemed to know when Chip didn't want meat and when, like now, he was happy to see a fat slice of ham sticking out around the edges of her golden-brown bread.

After lunch they put their dishes in the sink and went out to sit in the porch swing. The afternoon heat, combined with their full bellies, seemed to take away their energy to do anything. After a while, though, Chip began to feel restless.

"We should've stayed and played ball with Justin and Booker," he said. When Luther didn't answer, Chip added, "We need to practice more if we're going to try for the seventh-grade baseball team next year."

Luther shrugged. "It's not the varsity team anyway. Can't go out for that till ninth."

"Yeah, but nobody gets picked for the varsity team unless they did well in junior high."

Luther's glasses had slipped down a little on his nose. He pushed them back into place with one finger. "I'm not going out for baseball," he said without looking at Chip.

Chip was so surprised he planted both feet on the floor and stopped the swing in midmotion. "Why not? I mean, you being Booker Wilson's nephew, everybody'll be expecting—"

"That's why," Luther interrupted. "Everybody will expect me to be as good as he was."

Chip opened his mouth to protest, but Luther kept talking. "Think about it, Chip. Only two people in our school ever got put on the varsity baseball team as freshmen. The first one was Uncle Booker, more than twenty years ago, and the second was your brother."

"We don't have to be as good as they were," Chip argued. "We just have to be good enough to make the team. Which we can be, if we practice."

Luther picked up a book called *Jakeman* from the wicker table at the end of the swing. Chip had read it and hadn't found the story that interesting, but Luther liked it a lot, partly because it was set in New York, where he used to live. Luther flipped through it, not really paying attention to what was on the pages. For a minute Chip thought he had won the argument. Then Luther looked up and shoved his glasses back into place again. Chip could see he was still thinking serious thoughts. "That's another thing," Luther said.

"What?"

"Even when you're a natural like Uncle Booker and Justin, you have to practice all the time to be a star. Put everything you've got into getting good at that one thing. You know, like Lily. When do you ever see her without a soccer ball? She'd carry one to class if they'd let her."

Chip laughed. "Justin was like that too, remember? No matter what he was doing—walking, running, standing still— he was always tossing a baseball around. He had this thing where he used to lie in bed at night and throw the ball just so

25

it almost touched the ceiling. Over and over, millions of times. I can remember falling to sleep watching that ball spinning up and down, up and down."

Luther sat there thinking. "Thing is, Chip, I don't want to do just one thing. I like to read. I like helping Grandpa in his workshop. I like working in Grandma's garden, especially the seed-planting part, and watching the sprouts come up through the dirt. I don't want to go to ball practice every single day. Especially when everybody's going to be saying how I'm not as good as my Uncle Booker was."

It wasn't until Luther said all this out loud that Chip realized it was something his friend had been mulling over for a long time. After Luther's long speech—which was about the most words Chip had ever heard Luther say at one time—Chip thought about how he liked doing a lot of things too. He was never going to put in the kind of time Justin had put in to get good at baseball. And anyone who'd say that Luther wasn't as good as his uncle would say the same thing about Chip, because he'd never be as good as his brother. Still, he liked baseball. He was used to Justin being better, and it didn't really bother him.

"I want to learn to play something too. Music, I mean," Luther said.

Chip cut him a sharp look. Some of the community center kids were into rap, and a few times Chip had noticed Luther hanging around the edges of their group, watching them dance. Was that the kind of music Luther meant? Or was he talking about playing in the school band? If so, that wasn't going to leave much time for hanging out together.

The music part came as a surprise to Chip, but the next thing Luther said surprised him even more.

"If I did go out for a sport in seventh grade, I wish it could be soccer."

"You could," Chip offered, trying to sound encouraging.

Luther's shoulders slumped. "I don't think so. Look at how Lily gets around me when we play with her. I'm not anywhere near as good as she is."

Chip laughed. "Luther, nobody in sixth grade is as good as Lily. But you're good enough to make the team. She'd help you." Chip didn't add that it was easy to make the soccer team because it wasn't at the same level as the baseball team and there wasn't much competition. Also, he had intentionally said *you* and not *we* because he didn't plan to give up baseball to play soccer. Especially if it meant being bossed around by Lily.

Luther didn't answer. Chip was about to suggest that they walk back to the community center, thinking that the ball game was likely to go on all afternoon. But before Chip could come up with a good way to convince him, Luther got up from the swing and asked, "Want to walk over to the Old Place and count the rabbits?"

Counting rabbits at the Old Place was something they had been doing for three years, ever since they'd rescued a big white rabbit from an abusive owner. Not long after they let Mr. Rabbit loose at the Old Place, they found out it was actually *Miz* Rabbit. She had six babies in the first litter, but by now they'd lost track of how many litters Miz Rabbit had had. There were dozens of rabbits around the Old Place, and it was fun to see how many they could count in a single afternoon.

Chip and Luther ambled down Lost Goat Lane, then turned off onto a dirt track. The Old Place stood out from the cornfields surrounding it because it was the only place out here where there were any trees. The farmhouse had burned down decades ago, and not much was left but the foundations and a brick chimney so covered in morning glory vines that the faded red bricks were barely visible. A little way off was a barn with a caved-in roof, and next to the barn, a broken-down pen.

Behind the barn was what used to be a pasture, but now it was so heavily overgrown with thornbushes that it was almost impossible to walk through it. Beyond the bramble-filled pasture was ten acres of woods. Once Chip and Luther had tried to explore back there, but they hadn't gone more than a dozen yards when they hit a swampy area and sank up to their knees in mud. Then, while trying to get their feet out of the mud without losing their sneakers, they'd seen a coral snake. Luther had wanted to look at it up close, but Chip knew it was poison by the order of the colored bands. He'd taught Luther this verse on the spot: "Red by black, don't worry, Jack. Red by yellow, kill a fellow."

After that Chip and Luther referred to the woods as "the Jungle" and never went back. Instead, they checked out other things on the Old Place, like rabbit burrows in the thorn patch, the orange tree where a mockingbird always built her nest, and the barn owls that nested in the barn loft.

There were two good ways to count rabbits. Either you could climb the rickety ladder up into the loft and spot them from above, or you could lie in the grass in what had been the old cow pen and wait for the rabbits to come out into the open. The original Miz Rabbit wasn't afraid of the boys, and maybe she told her babies that that these humans wouldn't hurt them. The young ones were wilder than Miz Rabbit, but if Chip and Luther put out a few handfuls of grain and waited, they would come nibble at it.

The only trouble with trying to count rabbits, either from the ground or the loft, was that there were so many and they looked so much alike. All were either white like Miz Rabbit or brown like their swamp rabbit papa. Since they hopped all over the place, after a while you'd get mixed up, not sure which ones you had counted and which ones you hadn't.

Chip and Luther first climbed up into the loft to check out the view. This part of South Florida was about as flat as land could get. Looking through holes where boards had fallen off the walls, they could see the fields all around, as far as the Wilson place in one direction and, in the other direction, as far as Chip's house and the highway. What they didn't see on this particular afternoon was a lot of rabbits. A few dozen at most. Normally they'd see way more than that on a nice day like this.

After about fifteen minutes in the loft, Luther started sneezing from all the dust. "Let's get out of here," he said. "If we put out grain, more will come."

They climbed back down the ladder and went into the old cow pen. Luther dug into his pocket for the goat feed he'd brought along for just this purpose. After making a line of feed on the ground, the two boys sprawled on the grass and waited. Within a few minutes rabbits started hopping up. Soon there were about thirty-five, in all sizes, nibbling at the grain.

"Not as many as usual," Luther commented.

"More will come," Chip said. More always did if they waited long enough.

Both boys were quiet for a while, until suddenly Luther said in a low, angry voice, "I am *not* going to move away and leave all this."

Chip didn't know what to say, so at first he didn't say anything. Then it occurred to him that maybe Luther would feel better if he knew that they might be in the same boat. "You won't believe this," Chip said, trying to give Luther something to think about besides moving to town, "but it looks like Booker and Mom are stuck on each other. If they decided to get married and move somewhere else, we might both have to run away. Maybe we could come live here, in our hideout."

"That's crazy!" Luther snapped.

"What's crazy?" Chip sat up and tossed a dirt clod at Luther.

Luther threw it back at him. "Uncle Booker would never marry your mother in a million years!"

"Oh yeah? Then how come just last night he brought her flowers? *And* kissed her?"

Luther stood up, looking like he'd been punched in the stomach. "That doesn't mean they plan to get married." Luther could barely choke out the words.

"No," Chip admitted, "but they might." He added with a grin, "I wouldn't mind having Booker for a stepdad."

"You don't *need* a dad," Luther said angrily. "You've already got one."

"Not really," Chip said with a sudden rush of feelings that made his chest feel tight the way it always did when he thought about Charlie. "He's only been back to visit a few times since he and Mom got divorced. And then he spent most of the time with Justin. Now that Justin's not at home any-more, I'll probably never see him again."

Chip sat in the grass looking up at Luther. He knew Luther would understand how it felt to have a father who didn't care enough about you to stick around. After all, Luther's dad hadn't even stuck around till he was born.

But Luther didn't seem to have heard what Chip said. He was staring down at Chip with a look of pure fury.

"*You—listen—to—me!*" Luther said, jabbing his finger at Chip with each word. "Uncle Booker is *my uncle*. Not your dad. Not now and not ever!"

With that, Luther flung himself through the broken-down rails of the pen and tore off down the dirt track toward home.

Chip scrambled to his feet and, stopping just long enough to unsnag his T-shirt from one of the broken rails, ran out to the road. "Luther!" he yelled. "Wait!"

Luther didn't stop, so Chip took a deep breath and yelled as loud as he could, "I'm sorry!" And he was, even though he wasn't sure what for.

But Luther didn't even slow down.

5
Goodbye, Friend

Chip could have caught up to Luther—if not on the road, then at the house. But it was obvious that Luther didn't want to be caught, and Chip wasn't sure he wanted to catch him. In the four years of their friendship they'd had a few squabbles, but none of them had left Chip with such a mix-up of bad feelings. This was like having a headache and a stomachache and a bee sting all at the same time, and not knowing if you were more surprised or sad or mad. So instead of going after Luther, Chip walked home slowly and thought about the situation.

What Luther had said about Booker being *his* uncle made it sound like he wanted to keep Booker to himself or something—like if Booker got to be part of Chip's family, he wouldn't still be part of Luther's. That was just plain silly!

What worried Chip was that if Booker and Mom got married, they might decide to live in Atlanta, which was far away and would make it practically impossible for him and Luther to go on doing things together.

So they *did* have a problem—just not the one his friend thought they did. Or maybe it wasn't a problem. If Luther hadn't gotten mad and run off like that, they could've talked it over and might've decided it was nothing to worry about.

Chip hadn't kissed very many girls, but he knew that one lit-tle kiss didn't mean you were thinking about getting married!

When Chip reached his driveway, Booker's van was there. Through the kitchen window he could see Mom, Kate, and Ruby moving around. Everyone was laughing, almost like there was a party going on. It wasn't a party, though. Booker just had a way of laughing that made other people laugh too.

Chip detoured out to the duck pen to feed his quackers and gather the eggs, then went in through the back door. Booker's wheelchair was parked at the kitchen table, and Justin was sit-ting across from him. Kate and Ruby were stacking boxes of candy at one end of the counter. Mom, just home from work, was washing her hands at the sink.

Everyone turned and smiled at Chip. For half a second he felt a whole lot better. Then Ruby asked where Luther was and the good feeling disappeared.

"He went home," Chip said.

"Oh," Ruby said, turning back to the candy boxes.

Chip knew Ruby was probably thinking Luther had gone home just to avoid her. He wished he could explain to Ruby that she wasn't the one Luther was mad at right now. But the whole thing was too complicated, so he silently slid into the chair between Booker and Justin.

Mom bent over to take a roast out of the oven. "Mmmm! Doesn't that look good! Kate, you timed it just right!" She straightened up with the sizzling roast in her mitted hands. Kate slid the cutting board toward her so she'd have some-thing to put it on.

"Uh...Betty," Ruby said, giving her an apologetic look, "I think I won't stay for dinner after all."

Chip could see that Mom was surprised. "I—I thought we might all have supper here," she said. "But—"

33

"But Luther's not here," Ruby said softly. "I need to have a talk with my boy."

Ruby and Mom both looked at Booker, like they were asking him a question.

Booker hesitated a second, then backed his wheelchair away from the table. "Reckon I ought to have dinner with the folks tonight too." Then, speaking just to Mom, he said, "I think Sis needs a little backup on this one."

"Yes, of course," Mom said, looking a little puzzled. "Besides," she added, "I've barely had a minute with Justin. This'll be my only chance if you're driving back tomorrow."

Ruby loaded her arms with boxes of chocolates and said, "Kate, help me carry this candy out to the van. If I get the boxes decorated tonight, we can catch a ride to town with Booker when he leaves tomorrow and we won't have to use the goat cart."

"You can leave some here for me to do," Kate offered.

"I'll stop by later, Betty," Booker said to Mom in a low voice. "Is that okay?"

"Sure." Mom gave him a big smile, then turned to Chip and Justin. "How about you boys lift Booker's chariot down the back steps?"

They helped Booker, then walked with him and Ruby to the van and waved goodbye. Chip could have told Ruby and Booker that it wouldn't do a lick of good for them to try to talk to Luther, not in the mood he was in right now. But if he had said that, they would have expected him to explain why, and that was something he couldn't do. Not when he didn't entirely understand it himself.

Back in the house Kate had the table set and Mom was slicing the roast. When they had started eating, Mom asked, "How did it go at the community center?"

Justin spoke up first. "The kids were okay, considering. You wouldn't believe what some of them have been through. One got separated from his parents and they haven't been located yet. Another kid's grandpa was in the hospital, and he died when the power went off. There was this one boy, Ruben—not a bad ballplayer—who got trapped with his mom in the attic of their house. The whole downstairs was flooded and they had no food or water. He said it was like an oven up there in the attic. It was five days before somebody came in a boat and rescued them."

"Unbelievable!" Mom exclaimed. "I'm sure they all want to get on with their lives, but when so much changes all at once and you lose everything, I guess it's hard to know where to start." She turned to Chip. "How about you? Did the little ones enjoy the goat cart?"

Chip told them about the three-year-old who'd had to leave her goat behind because the helicopter pilot didn't have time to rescue a goat, and how the girl hugged Billy so hard her mom had to pry her loose. Then Chip launched into the story of Old Billy and the hot dog buns. He rolled up a slice of bread and demonstrated how Billy had looked with the bun sticking out of his mouth. Everybody laughed, which lightened things up a little.

Then Mom said, "What did Booker mean when he said Ruby needed backup? Is Luther in some kind of trouble?"

"Luther's totally freaked out," Kate said.

At first Chip wondered how Kate knew that. Then he realized that Ruby had probably told her while they were boxing up the candy.

"About what?" Mom asked, giving Kate her full attention.

"Ruby and Mr. Jackson getting married."

"They *are?*" Mom asked in delight. "You mean he finally proposed?"

"Last night." Kate was obviously pleased that she'd heard about it before Mom. "Didn't she tell you?"

"How could she? I walked in the door not ten minutes before Chip got home. But, well—that's wonderful!"

"Luther doesn't think it's so wonderful," Chip said.

"What's his problem with Mr. Jackson?" Justin asked, spearing another piece of roast beef. "He was a better teacher than some of the professors I've got now."

"It's not him," Chip explained. "It's having to move to Mr. Jackson's place."

"Oh." Mom leaned back in her chair and looked at Chip. "Where does he live?"

"About a block from the school," Kate said. "In that new apartment complex."

"That's a nice place," Mom said. "I can see how they'd want to live there after the wedding."

For a minute it was quiet except for the sound of silverware clanking and people chewing. Chip tried to swallow a bite of potato, but for some reason it stuck in his throat. He had to take a swig of milk to wash it down. He looked at his mother. "Would you?"

"Would I what?"

"If you got married, would you want to move?"

Mom laughed, but her eyes were serious. "It wouldn't make much sense for me to move, now that the mortgage is paid off and we own this place outright. It's different for Ruby, living with her parents. She and Richard would naturally want a home of their own."

"Luther likes things the way they are," Chip said, almost under his breath. Nobody answered, so Chip mumbled "'Scuse me" and got up to clear the table.

"I'll wash dishes tonight, twerp," Justin said. "You can have a holiday."

"What a nice offer." Mom beamed at Justin. "And I'll dry, to give Kate a holiday."

"Thanks," said Kate, rushing out of the kitchen before Mom changed her mind.

Chip figured that Mom had volunteered so she could have a few minutes to talk to Justin about how things were going for him in college.

Instead of feeling good about getting out of washing the dishes, Chip scuffed down the hall feeling mad at Luther all over again. If it hadn't been for Luther, Chip would have stayed at the community center and played ball with Justin. He'd missed his chance to spend time with his brother then, and he wasn't getting to spend time with him now. And tomorrow Justin would be leaving!

As Chip passed Kate's bedroom he saw her standing at the dresser with her back to him. She must have seen him in the mirror because she turned around. "Chip? You okay?"

"What do you mean?" he asked grumpily.

"I don't know. You look—" She didn't say what he looked like, but came and put her arm around his shoulder. She hadn't done that in years, not since she used to have to babysit him all the time. Nowadays Kate pretty much lived in her own world. At home she was always busy with chores and homework and the chocolate and clothes businesses she and Ruby had started. At school she was preoccupied with her boyfriend, Brad, and the school newspaper they both worked on.

"Are you having problems at school?" Kate asked.

Chip wondered why adults—and Kate when she was in her substitute-mom mode—never seemed to realize that kids had other problems besides school. Instead of answering, he asked, "You going out again tonight?"

"Brad's coming by to pick me up in about half an hour. Justin's coming too."

"I thought Mom said she didn't want you spending so much time with Brad."

Kate shrugged impatiently. "That's only when Justin's not here. She never minds when it's the three of us. Anyway, her excuse was that going steady would hurt my grades. I aced *all* my midterms, so what excuse has she got now?"

"Well, have fun," Chip said gloomily. He headed down the hall toward his room. "I got homework."

"We're not leaving for a while," Kate called after him. "Let me know if you need any help."

Chip didn't need any help. In fact, he didn't even need to do his homework. It was only Saturday night. Usually he waited till the last minute, even though it meant doing without TV all weekend, because one of Mom's rules was no TV until your homework was done. But if he did his assignments right now, he could watch TV later tonight.

He finished in time to watch the last half of a movie. Then he took a shower and got into bed. He had just turned out the light when Booker's van drove up. Chip looked out the window. Booker just sat there. After a couple of minutes Mom walked out to the van. Chip was wondering if he should go down and help her bring Booker's wheelchair up the steps when she opened the door and climbed into the van.

Chip could see the outline of their heads as they sat there in the van's bucket seats. Even though his window was open and the van windows were open, he couldn't hear what they were saying. *Maybe they're talking about Luther,* he thought. After a few minutes Booker laughed, and then Mom laughed. Chip smiled. Nobody was better at getting people in a good mood than Booker. If Booker went home to help Ruby talk to Luther, Chip figured the problem was as good as solved.

Chip climbed back into bed. The last thing he remembered before falling asleep was thinking that by tomorrow Luther would be back to his normal self and they could have a serious discussion about what sport they wanted to play next year.

6
Two Rotten Weeks

Chip slept in on Sunday morning, but eventually the baaing of the goats wanting to be milked nagged him out of bed. The Martins used to have only one milk goat, Brown Sugar. Now Sugar's daughters, Honey and Go-Girl, also had to be milked. Mom bought the feed for all the goats and kept Brown Sugar's milk for the family. They sold the milk from Honey (who belonged to Kate) and Go-Girl (who belonged to Chip) to families in town whose children were allergic to cow milk. Kate and Chip liked that arrangement because it gave them a little extra spending money. The only downside was having to milk the goats twice a day, but normally Chip did the morning milking and Kate took the evening. Chip got dressed and headed out to the goat pen.

On weekends, Chip usually hurried through his chores and then ran over to the Wilsons' farm. This morning he was hoping that if he dawdled, Luther would show up at his place the way he often did when Chip was running late. But Luther didn't come. Chip went in the house, put away the fresh milk, and fixed himself a bowl of cereal. Kate was hogging the kitchen table, where she was busy decorating the last of the candy boxes, so Chip broke one of Mom's rules and carried his bowl of cereal into the living room. Justin came in with a huge armload of laundry fresh from the dryer. He dropped it on the couch next to Chip and started rolling underwear and T-shirts and jeans and stuffing everything into a duffel bag.

"How come you're rolling your clothes instead of folding them?" Chip asked.

"Fits better," Justin said.

Chip watched him for a minute then asked, "Do you like living in Atlanta?"

"Don't know. Being in college there is not exactly like living there."

"I don't get it. If you don't live *there*, where *do* you live?"

Justin stirred through the pile of clothes, looking for a mate to one of his socks. "Nowhere, I guess."

"That's stupid." Chip picked up the missing sock from the floor and tossed it to Justin. "Everybody lives somewhere."

"Not necessarily," Justin retorted, rolling the two socks together and flipping them into the duffel bag. "Just because you're staying somewhere doesn't mean you *live* there. Like the kids at the community center. They sort of live there, but not really, not the way you live here. They're in transition, between where they used to live and wherever they're going next."

"What about you?" Chip asked.

"I don't know where I'm going next either," Justin admitted. "But at least I'll always have this place if I want to come back. Nothing ever changes around here."

"Maybe you'll want to stay in Atlanta," Chip persisted, hoping Justin would say he'd never want to live there and would have a fit if Mom even thought about selling the farm.

But all Justin said was, "Maybe." He glanced at the clock. "Booker'll be here any minute. If I don't get a move on it, I'll be *walking* to Atlanta."

Justin had just closed the zipper on the bag when Booker's van drove up. Kate called from the kitchen, "Chip, would you come help me carry this candy out to the van?"

Chip had been thinking all morning that maybe Luther was waiting to catch a ride with Booker to the Martins' house. But there was no Luther in the van. Justin flung his duffel bag in the van's luggage area and got in the front next to Booker. Kate and Ruby sat in the backseat with the candy stacked carefully between them. They all waved a cheery goodbye, and off they went. Chip waved back, barely able to hold his smile in place.

He went down to the drainage ditch that ran along the side of the pasture and watched the ducks paddling around. When some of them waddled up to him doing their quack-quack thing with their big yellow bills, Chip reached in his pocket to see if he had anything for them. He pulled out the end of yesterday's stale hot dog bun and tossed it into the water bit by bit. Watching the ducks dive for the crumbs made him smile. But it didn't make him happy.

Then, without even deciding to do it, Chip got up and went down Lost Goat Lane to Luther's house. When he knocked on the front door, Mrs. Wilson answered. She said Luther was in his room and not feeling good, but she would ask if he felt like company.

She came back in a minute. "I'm sorry, Chip. Luther says he doesn't want any company right now."

"It's okay," Chip mumbled, and turned to leave. "Just tell him…I mean…tell him it's okay."

Mrs. Wilson came out onto the porch and put her arm around his shoulder. "You know, Chip, Luther is very upset about his mama's plans to move to town after she gets married. I expect he'll get over it, but it might take a little while."

"Yes'm." Mrs. Wilson was the only one who seemed to

understand that it wasn't Ruby getting married that upset Luther. It was the idea of moving. But even Mrs. Wilson didn't know what else Luther was mad about.

When Chip got to the bus stop the next morning, he saw Luther in the distance, walking slowly up Lost Goat Lane. Luther and Chip had been waiting for that school bus together ever since the first day of second grade. But Chip could tell that Luther intended to poke along until the bus got there, then make a dash for it. That way he wouldn't have to talk to Chip.

"Come on, Luther!" Lily yelled when the bus pulled up. "You wanna have to walk?"

Lily got on first, followed by Chip. He took his usual seat just ahead of Lily and slid over by the window, leaving space for Luther. When Luther finally got on, the bus driver barked at him for fooling around. Looking at the floor, Luther walked down the aisle past Chip and Lily and flopped into a seat near the back.

When the bus stopped at their school, things got worse. Chip waited for Luther to get off, but his friend walked right past him and went over to join Ruben and some other boys from the community center. Chip figured Luther was using them to get away from him, so he stayed by himself and acted like he didn't care.

Luther managed to avoid Chip all day, even at lunch. That afternoon when Chip got on the bus, Luther was already sitting next to Lily. They didn't even look up when Chip walked past. Chip heard something about a corner kick and figured they were talking about soccer.

When the bus stopped to let them off, Luther and Lily were so heavy into their soccer conversation that neither of them noticed when Chip brushed past. He didn't walk away fast, like he was mad or anything, because he wasn't. He stopped once to throw stones over the power line. He was almost to his driveway when he heard feet running after him.

"Chip!" Lily called. "Wait!"

He turned around. "What?"

"Luther wants to work on soccer skills. Want to come over to my place?"

"No thanks," Chip mumbled. "I got homework."

"Oh," Lily said. "Too bad. Will you take this then?"

As she dug into the pocket of her soccer shorts, Chip knew it would be something she'd saved from lunch, and it would be for Honey, the smallest of the original goat triplets and therefore Lily's favorite. She shoved some celery sticks in Chip's hand, along with some crumbled corn chips.

He took the goat snacks and started to walk away. Then he turned back. "You could practice in our yard. There's more space."

"I suggested that, but Luther wants to practice at my house," Lily said.

Chip watched as she ran back to where Luther was waiting. He kept his eyes on them until they dashed across the highway together and disappeared behind some cars in the nursery parking lot.

That was how the whole rest of the week went. Luther hung out with the kids from the community center at school and went over to Lily's to practice soccer after school. On the bus ride to and from school, Lily and Luther sat together and talked soccer.

The following week things changed, but not for the better. On Tuesday afternoon Luther and Lily weren't on the bus. He was wondering where they were when Tamara, a girl he used to like in fifth grade, moved from the seat across the aisle and sat down by him. Even though Chip had stopped liking her a long time ago, he was glad she'd sat next to him. But the moment Tamara slid into the seat, she looked over at the girl she'd been sitting with and the two of them started giggling like crazy. Chip realized that Tamara had probably sat by him on a dare. He turned away from her and stared out the window.

It was because he was staring out the window that Chip found out why Luther and Lily weren't on the bus. The bus had only gone a couple of blocks when he saw them walking with the kids from the community center. It only took Chip two seconds to figure out that Luther had made friends with them and had talked them into accepting Lily. Now they were all one big happy soccer-playing family, and Chip was the odd man out.

He folded his arms on the window ledge and laid his head on his hands. He hadn't felt this miserable since the summer his little dog Go-Boy was eaten by an alligator.

7
Biology

During those first two weeks after Luther stopped being his friend, Chip dreaded going to school. The only hour of the day that was bearable was science class. Chip used to think of science as a bunch of boring words in a textbook, but Mr. O'Dell had changed all that. And kind of by accident, Chip had become one of Mr. O'Dell's favorite students.

It started when Mr. O'Dell announced how students could get a good grade in his class—not by memorizing a lot of facts but by *thinking*. The students stared at him, either wondering what he was talking about or else marveling at the fringe of reddish brown hair surrounding his shiny bald head.

"What do you mean by 'thinking'?" somebody asked.

Mr. O'Dell had answered by asking another question. "What common substance can take the form of a liquid, a solid, or a gas?"

Nobody answered. The class just sat there, waiting for Mr. O'Dell to explain what that had to do with anything. Then Chip got it. Mr. O'Dell meant that he was likely to throw out questions about things that weren't in the book and expect students to figure out the answers for themselves. To Chip the question seemed more like a riddle.

The first liquid Chip thought of was water, and then he thought of ice. Ice is a solid. And when water gets super hot, it turns to steam. He wasn't sure if steam was a gas or not, but when nobody else spoke, Chip blurted out, "Water?"

After that Chip could tell that Mr. O'Dell liked him. Chip liked him too—at least most of the time. In English, social studies, and math, Mr. O'Dell was just an average teacher. But the minute the lesson turned to science, Mr. O'Dell practically exploded with energy and enthusiasm.

The best part about science class was the field trips. The principal usually allowed outdoor field trips only once or twice a semester, but Mr. O'Dell had special permission to take his class once a month to a big vacant lot down the street to study biology "in the field." Kate had told Chip that Mr. O'Dell had once taught in college and had written a book on field biology. She figured that was the reason he got special privileges.

Chip quickly discovered that what Mr. O'Dell called field biology was what he had been doing all his life: paying attention to other living things. Chip had favorites—ducks and turtles, for example, and lightning bugs. But Mr. O'Dell seemed to be interested in every living creature. Once when a student pointed out an anthill, Mr. O'Dell put his nose down so close to watch that Chip expected an ant to climb right onto it and march up through the freckles to stare back at him through his gold-rimmed glasses. Another time, Mr. O'Dell had the whole class sit cross-legged in a circle to watch a chameleon change from brown to bright green. While they waited still and quiet, they got to see it let down a flap of bright red skin under its chin to attract insects. Anyone who wasn't paying close attention missed the important moment when the lizard flicked out its long tongue and whisked a fly back into its mouth.

Mr. O'Dell had the students take detailed notes on each animal or insect they were observing. He also encouraged them to make sketches of what they saw. The trips with Mr. O'Dell had taught Chip a different way of looking at things.

Out where Chip lived there wasn't a lot of wildlife in the plowed fields, which were heavily pesticided. But quite a few interesting creatures still lived in the drainage ditches and the high grass along the banks. When Luther first came to live with his grandparents, Chip had showed him where to find the birds' nests built so low to the ground that you could look right in and watch the eggs hatch. He'd also taught Luther—a boy raised in New York City who knew nothing about Florida wildlife—how to tell the difference between slow land turtles and snapping turtles. For one thing, if you didn't catch a snapping turtle just right, it could give you a bite that really hurt.

From the beginning, there was one difference in the way Chip and Luther dealt with the wildlife they came across. Whatever it was, Chip wanted to catch it. But Luther always said, "No! It's scared. Let it go." So Chip usually did.

Mr. O'Dell never talked about an animal's feelings, but about its purpose, and why it ought to be right where it was, doing whatever it was doing. Like the day after Luther got mad at Chip, when Chip brought a blue skink to class. Mr. O'Dell was as excited as if it was a baby dinosaur. In about five minutes he had everybody in the class involved in trying to find out more about skinks. But when the class ended, he'd called Chip up to his desk and said, "Now, you'll take this skink back and put it right where you found it, won't you?"

Chip stared at him in surprise. "If you don't want him, I can just let him go outside the school."

Mr. O'Dell looked at the skink, then at Chip. "If somebody put you in a car and drove you far away and dumped you out, would that be okay with you?"

"Probably not," Chip admitted. "I'd want to go home."

"Most critters do," Mr. O'Dell pointed out. "Things do happen that displace us from our homes. Humans are pretty good at adapting to new locations, but even for them it's stressful. And some creatures can't manage it at all. If you take them out of their natural environment, they just die."

Chip stared at the skink until Mr. O'Dell asked, "Do you understand?"

"Yes sir." But Chip wasn't thinking about the skink. He was thinking about Luther, not wanting to leave the environment he was used to. Maybe that was why Luther had started hanging out with the kids at the community center. Maybe he thought they'd understand how it felt to be about to lose your home, since they'd already lost theirs.

Chip took the skink back to the drainage ditch where he'd found it and let it go.

8
The Birthday Party

On Thursday afternoon of the second rotten week, Lily got on the bus like she would have before she and Luther started being soccer buddies. She plopped down in the seat next to Chip and said, "Hi."

"Hi," Chip said. He almost asked where Luther was but decided not to. A few minutes later he knew the answer anyway, because he saw Luther walking along the street with Ruben and some other community center kids.

"How come you're not going with them to play soccer?" Chip asked.

"Can't," Lily said. "Dentist appointment."

"Oh." Chip wondered if Luther had told Lily why he was mad at him. If so, she didn't mention it.

Giving him a serious look, she said, "Chip, I know you don't care that much for soccer because you're planning to go out for the baseball team next year. But for now, well, it's better to play *some* sport, isn't it? I mean, you need to keep in shape and all that."

"Yeah, so?"

"So you ought to start coming to the community center and playing soccer with us after school. Just to keep your reflexes sharp."

"Why there?" Chip asked peevishly. "I thought you didn't like those kids."

Lily looked at him in surprise. "Didn't Luther tell you?"

"What?"

"He promised Booker he'd spend some time with them. You know, so they wouldn't feel so out of it during the time they're stuck here."

"Oh," Chip said. "So it was Luther's idea to start playing soccer with them?"

"Yeah. But it was a good idea. With just him and me, all we can do is skills practice. With the community center kids, there are enough for two teams. Plus, one of the dads at the center referees for us. It's a lot better to play with a referee."

Lily reached into her shorts pocket and pulled out a bag of corn chips. She bit open the top of the bag and held it out for him to take some. Then she poured herself a handful and sat there crunching on them. "At least you should come with us after school tomorrow. You don't have to play soccer if you don't want to."

"Why tomorrow?" Chip asked.

"It's the birthday party."

"Whose birthday?"

"Three different kids, but we're just getting one big cake. Ruben's friend Ralph is turning thirteen, and then there's this really shy boy. Chip, you aren't going to believe what happened to him. His family's house in Mexico got destroyed in a hurricane, so they came to Florida to stay with an aunt on the Gulf Coast. They hadn't even been there a month when that other hurricane roared through and wrecked her house! Now they don't know where to go."

"Wow!" Chip said. "That's terrible." Then he asked, "Who's the third person?"

"Saralee. That little girl who kept hugging Old Billy, remember? The one who had to leave her own goat behind? She's turning four. It's not going to be a party with presents. Just cake and ice cream and some balloons."

When Chip still didn't say anything, Lily asked, "So, will you come?"

"When is it?" Chip asked.

"Right after school. My mom's going to pick up the cake, then she'll come by and pick up Luther and me. And you, if you want to come."

"Okay," Chip said finally.

"Good," Lily said. "Lucky we won't have Old Billy with us. He didn't actually like those hot dog buns, but I bet he'd really go for birthday cake."

The moment they got to the center, Lily and Luther joined Ruben and his friends at the refreshment tables. Chip volunteered to help out with the activities for the little kids. While he was blowing up balloons, Saralee came over and asked him where his goat was. He said it was at home. "So's mine," she said sadly. "On the roof all by herself." Chip wondered if the little girl thought the goat was still there waiting for her to come back.

Chip blew up the biggest balloon he could find and used a magic marker to draw a goat on the balloon. He wasn't the world's greatest artist, but Saralee recognized it as a goat. When he handed her the balloon, she laughed and ran to her mother, screaming, "Mama, look! I got a goat balloon!"

Chip looked after her, feeling glad he had come. So glad that he even smiled and said, "Happy birthday!" to Ralph when he wandered over for a second piece of cake.

Ralph was one of the bigger boys who had pushed Lily down during that first soccer game. He'd looked pretty tough at the time—tough enough that Chip had been scared of him. But now, wearing a big happy grin and stuffing birthday cake in his mouth, Ralph looked harmless enough.

When the happy birthday part of the party was over, Lily started herding the older kids toward the soccer field. She saw that Chip wasn't following, so she came over to the balloon table. "Come on, Chip," she urged. "I want you on my team!"

"What about Luther?" he asked.

"He's on Ruben's team." She grinned. "But you know Miguel, that seventh grader from Mexico? He's on mine. He's awesome."

Chip wasn't normally the competitive type. But all of a sudden he wanted to get out there on the field and do everything in his power to see his team win and Luther's lose. As Chip walked onto the field with Lily, he saw Luther watching him out of the corner of his eye and knew that he felt exactly the same.

"You play defense," Lily said.

Chip thought she could have at least asked if he *wanted* to play defense. In after-school games they usually played all over, in no particular position. Chip didn't argue, though. He just went where Lily pointed, on the left side of the field.

All five goals that Ruben's team scored in the first half came from the right. Two of the attackers on Chip's side of the field were bigger and faster than he was, but Chip was good at guessing where the ball would go and usually got to it before they did. If he hadn't, Lily's team would have been down by a much bigger margin. It also helped that Miguel, who always seemed to be in the open waiting for a pass, had scored three goals for their team.

At halftime, some of the kids' mothers brought over oranges cut in quarters and a cooler of water. Even though the other team was leading, Chip felt good about how well he had played. Luther and his teammates were clustered together about twenty yards away. They seemed to be feeling pretty good too, probably because they were ahead by two goals.

As soon as the second half started, Ruben scored another goal, but after that Miguel was really fired up. He scored three goals within ten minutes. Next Lily scored on an individual effort, getting the ball past three players before beating the goalie.

The game was almost over when Ruben fed Luther a perfect pass. Luther had a chance to score a goal to make it a tie. Without thinking, Chip flung his body sideways feetfirst so his legs were between the ball and the goal. Luther, who was trying to kick the ball when it was suddenly blocked, tumbled forward. His glasses flew off and went bouncing along behind him.

"You okay?" Chip asked as the referee's whistle signaled the end of the game.

"You fouled me!" Luther said angrily. He got up and stomped back to get his glasses.

"No, he didn't!" Lily yelled. "That was perfectly legal!"

Just then Mrs. Hashimoto drove into the parking lot and honked. Lily picked up her soccer ball and whacked Chip on the back. "See? I told you we could do it." To Miguel she said, "I sure hope you're still here next year when I get to seventh grade. We could be the best junior high soccer team this school has ever had."

Luther was standing off to one side with Ruben and a couple of other big boys from the center. "Let's go, Luther," Lily called, "before my mom has a conniption fit."

"I'll walk home," Luther said. "I'm going to play some more. With my friends."

Just like that, Chip's good feeling from blocking Luther's goal shot vanished, and the misery of having lost his best friend for practically no reason came rushing back.

9
The Jungle

When Chip got up on Saturday morning, Mom was long gone and Kate was on the phone, holding a fashion magazine in one hand. "I know you don't want a formal wedding, Ruby, but you won't believe this dress," she raved. "It is *gorgeous*. And we can make it ourselves!"

The last thing Chip wanted to hear about was weddings. He went to the kitchen and poured himself a bowl of cereal.

"I'm going down to the Wilsons'," Kate called after a minute. "Want to come?"

"No thanks." Chip grabbed the milk out of the fridge and sat down at the table.

"Oh, right," Kate said on her way toward the back door. "You and Luther had a fight, didn't you?"

Chip gave her a you-don't-know-anything look and didn't bother to answer.

Kate shrugged in an exaggerated way and said, "Sorrrry!" Then the screen door slammed and she was gone.

After doing his chores, Chip headed for the Old Place. Going there wasn't the same without Luther, but it would be better than hanging around the house doing nothing.

Walking toward the Old Place and looking at it from a distance, Chip remembered that time he and Luther had gone into the woods on the back side of the property. They'd bush-whacked through the thorny brambles that covered what used to be the pasture behind the old barn. They hadn't thought about entering the woods from this side, because there's no road back there. Also, drainage ditches divided the Old Place from the fields around it. Chip and Luther were too little then to jump one of the ditches to get across, but that was three years ago. Chip thought he might be able to do it now. And it would be fun to explore that part of the woods.

So instead of approaching the Old Place from the front, Chip turned left into the cornfield. He walked between the cornstalk rows until he was even with the thick woods he and Luther had called "the Jungle." He checked out the ditch sep-arating the cornfield from the woods. It was pretty wide and full of water, but he thought he could make it with a running start. He backed up between the cornstalks, sprinted toward the ditch, and took a mighty leap. He made it across, but he landed low on the opposite bank. It crumbled, leaving him among the cattails, hip-deep in ditch water. He scrambled out and up the bank on the other side. His heart was beating fast.

He was in the Jungle. Alone.

The ground between the cypress trees was soggy in some places and ankle-deep in water in others. Cypress knees stuck up everywhere. Chip had to pick his way through the swamp carefully, because it was easy to trip on the parts of the cypress roots that were under the water. He also had to keep his eye out for poisonous snakes. Cottonmouth water moccasins liked areas like this, not to mention the even more deadly coral snakes like the one that had scared the daylights out of him and Luther that day. So Chip moved slowly, giving the snakes, if there were any, time to get out of the way. The water got deeper, until it turned into a small pond with water that came up to his hips. Up ahead he could see a knoll covered in short green grass. It looked like solid ground.

Chip sloshed out of the water and sprawled on the grassy knoll, which was about as big as a small front yard. Long gray moss hung from some of the surrounding trees, and exotic-looking blossoms dangled from some of the branches. Chip didn't know much about flowers, but he thought they might be orchids. One thing he did know: This place was *beautiful.*

Chip lay in the grass, taking in his surroundings and breathing in the swampy smell. A bird swam across the pond, its body completely below the water. All Chip could see of it was a long neck and a head. It had speared a small fish with its sharp beak. The bird came to the surface and swallowed the fish. Then it flapped onto a dead branch and spread its wings to dry in the sun. The bird didn't seem to mind that Chip was there. He stayed perfectly still, the way Mr. O'Dell had taught his students to do when they were observing a creature in the wild. Chip got a good look at the bird, black with silvery white spots on its wings and back. He'd seen birds like that before, but not this close. He hadn't realized how big they were.

After a while the bird flew off. Chip moved to the edge of the water and peered in. Now that his feet weren't sloshing through it stirring up the mud, maybe he could see what kind of fish were there. And for the first time he wondered if there might be alligators in this swampy place. He walked along the knoll, looking very carefully at the narrow muddy strip between the grass and the water. If there were any alligators around, there would be places called slides, where the gators slid down the bank into the water.

It was because he was paying particular attention to the mud at the edge of the water that he saw the tracks. He knelt down to study them. Mr. O'Dell had taught his students how to tell the difference between dog and cat tracks. These were definitely cat tracks, but bigger than any Chip had ever seen. He studied the prints, wondering if there was a big tomcat living around here. Could that be what was happening to their rabbits? A feral tomcat wouldn't see any difference between eating a rat and eating a bunny.

Then Chip felt the hairs stand up on the back of his neck, giving him the feeling of being watched. He turned quickly, but there was nothing behind him but the grassy knoll and, beyond it, the woods.

It was midafternoon and he was getting hungry. He sloshed back across the swampy area, jumped the ditch into the cornfield, and trotted along between the cornstalks feeling as high as the sky. From now on he had a place to come, a private and beautiful place where he could forget about Luther for a while. Way out here in the swamp there wouldn't be anyone asking every five minutes, "Where's Luther?" or "Did you and Luther have a fight?" or, worst of all, "How's Luther feeling today?"

As if he should know.

On Sunday, Chip was up in time to say bye to Mom before she left for work. She'd been on the phone with Booker for more than an hour the night before. Chip had stood in the doorway between the kitchen and living room listening for a minute, but they didn't seem to be saying anything important. He didn't see any point in eavesdropping unless they were talking about him or Luther. One thing Chip had to admit as Mom waved goodbye and headed off toward the nursery: She was always a lot more cheerful after she'd been talking to Booker. But then, who wasn't?

Chip tried not to think about Mom and Booker anymore. If he hadn't felt so bad about telling Luther about them, he could have put them out of his head entirely. He made a sandwich, filled a thermos with water, and headed for the door.

Kate came in just then, still in pajamas, her blonde hair all frowsy. "Morning," she mumbled. "Where are you off to so early?"

"It's not that early," Chip countered, glancing at the clock, which showed a little after eight. "What are *you* doing up already? You and Brad were out pretty late."

"I'm *always* home by curfew," Kate said airily.

That was technically true, but she often sat out in the car with Brad talking (so she said) till after midnight. Chip knew she'd done that the night before, because he'd heard the car drive up, and it had been a good long time before he'd heard her come in the house.

"Ruby's coming over in a little while," Kate explained as she got some orange juice out of the fridge. "We're going do some modifications to this great wedding dress design I found in *Bride* magazine."

"How exciting," Chip said, letting the door bang shut behind him. It seemed impossible to have any kind of conversation with his family nowadays without being reminded of either Luther or weddings.

As soon as he started down Lost Goat Lane, he felt better. This was like running away from home, only better. As long as he did his chores and was home for supper, nobody would guess where he'd been.

Chip didn't jump the ditch where he had the day before. Instead, he walked all the way around to the back of the Old

Place to see if he could get into the woods from there. But the ditch on the back side was a lot wider—much too wide to jump. He circled back around until he found a place where the ditch was jumpable, then chose a solid takeoff spot, took a flying leap, and landed in a patch of ragweed as tall as he was. He was careful not to break down the soft ragweed stems, because he didn't want to disturb any red-winged blackbirds' nests. Many times he'd carefully bent back ragweed stalks and peered in to see the speckled eggs or baby birds in the nests.

Just beyond the ragweed that grew along the ditch the brush thinned out so it was easy walking. The ground was muddy in some places, but not swampy. He stopped often to look, listen, and smell. It was amazingly quiet.

Chip wandered around awhile before he found the grassy knoll and marshy pond. This time a big white bird with long legs stood alone in the marsh. Chip knew it was a heron, but it was bigger than the ones he often saw out in their pasture with the goats. Those small herons would light right on an animal's back and pick off the insects. This big white one used its beak to spear a fish, just like the big black bird he'd seen the day before.

Chip checked the muddy edge of the water and again found cat tracks. He sat down and ate his sandwich, staring at the tracks. He'd never had a cat—Mom was afraid a cat might go after the baby ducks—so Chip wasn't that familiar with the size of the average cat's paw. He was pretty sure, though, that this was a real fat cat. Or maybe a cat with extra-big feet? He couldn't figure out why the muddy strip next to the pond was so tracked up. As far as Chip knew, cats didn't swim. So why all the tracks next to the water? Had it come to get a drink? Did it live here in the meadow and had it run into the forest to hide when it heard him coming?

Chip moved into the shade and sat with his back against a tree, watching dragonflies hover over the swampy water. Now and then a bird landed in a nearby tree. The big black bird came back and sat on the same dead tree branch to dry its wings.

No doubt about it, this place was a real Garden of Eden. But Chip couldn't help feeling like Old Adam might have felt before Eve showed up: As good as it was, it would be a lot better if he had someone to share it with. More than once he almost said, "Hey, Luther! Look!" Then he'd remember—Luther wasn't there.

To get his mind on something else, he decided to do a little exploring. He glimpsed a small animal as it darted into a burrow. He thought it might be an armadillo, but he wasn't dumb enough to stick his hand down the hole to find out. He found a red-winged blackbird's nest in a bush and a bullbat's nest on the ground. The baby birds opened their mouths wide when he squatted to get a better look. It definitely would've been nice to share those things with his best friend. On the other hand, there was something special about being the only person who had ever seen them.

Chip left the Jungle the way he'd come in the day before, by wading through the swamp among the big cypress trees. By the time he jumped across the ditch and scrambled up into the cornfield, he had a map of the Jungle in his head. The pond and the grassy knoll were more or less in the middle. The easiest way to get there was from the other side, where the trees were farther apart and the ground wasn't so marshy.

10
The Intruder

Chip had just reached the road when something stopped him in his tracks. Lying in the grass near the crumbling foundations of the old house was a bicycle. He stared, wondering who it belonged to. Then he heard a sound that surprised him more than the sight of a strange bicycle.

"Ow!" The yelp came from behind the crepe myrtle and hibiscus bushes around the foundations of the old house. The bushes parted and a familiar face came bursting through, followed by a grown-up body wearing jeans and a T-shirt.

Chip's mouth dropped open. "Mr. O'Dell! What are you doing here?"

Mr. O'Dell didn't answer but started hopping around, slapping at his legs. Then he bent over and rolled up his pants legs. Chip could see several red welts on his teacher's calves. He figured that Mr. O'Dell had probably gotten so absorbed in watching an ant colony that he hadn't noticed when some of the warrior ants crawled up his leg—at least not until they started biting.

When Mr. O'Dell finally got the ants out of his pants, he straightened up and walked over to the bike. "Hi, Chip," he said, still rubbing his legs. "Do you live around here?"

"Yes sir." Chip pointed in the direction of his house. "Over by the highway."

"First time I've biked out here," Mr. O'Dell said. "Great place. Any idea who owns it?"

"The Franklin family," Chip said. "They don't live around here anymore, though. The house burned down a long time ago, even before my mom was born."

"That must explain why it's still in native vegetation," Mr. O'Dell said excitedly. "The back part, anyway. What a great place this would be to bring the class on a field trip!"

Chip's stomach turned to jelly. The idea of a bunch of kids running all over what had been his and Luther's hideout for four years almost made him sick. Even worse was the thought of someone else discovering his special secret place beyond the woods.

"If you live close by, you must have been here a few times." Mr. O'Dell sat down cross-legged by his bike and looked at the welts on his ankles. "Any idea what kind of ants these are? Boy, do they bite!"

"I don't know," Chip mumbled. "But there's some aloe vera around here. If you rub it on the bites, it helps. Want me to look for some?"

"That would be great. Thanks."

Chip wandered off to look for an aloe vera plant—and to give himself time to adjust to the sudden intrusion of Mr. O'Dell, who might be on the verge of dragging twenty-five kids out to the Old Place. If Mr. O'Dell decided to bring the class here, there wasn't much he could do about it. But maybe he could persuade Mr. O'Dell not to let anybody go into the woods. Maybe he could at least keep that area for himself. Chip returned with one of the fat aloe vera leaves and handed it to his teacher.

Mr. O'Dell broke open the thick leaf and smeared the jelly-like insides on the ant bites. While Chip watched him, a plan formed in his mind. He'd try to get Mr. O'Dell so interested in the area around the house and barn that he wouldn't notice the woods.

"There are lots of critters right around here. In that old barn," Chip said, pointing, "there's an owl's nest. It's up high, so you can't see inside it. But you can find really interesting things, like mice skulls and stuff, in the droppings on the ground under the nest."

Actually, it *was* possible to look into the nest. He and Luther and Lily had done it lots of times. But Chip didn't feel like telling Mr. O'Dell how they did it.

"Really!" Mr. O'Dell forgot about his ant bites and got excited again. "What else?"

"There are some birds' nests over there in the crepe myrtle bushes."

"I saw those." Mr. O'Dell went back to smearing aloe on his legs. "Anything else?"

"Well…" Chip hesitated. "There are rabbits." He nodded toward the overgrown pasture. "They make burrows under those bramble bushes. It's hard to get around in there because of the thorns, but the rabbits sometimes come out in the open."

"Really?" Mr. O'Dell looked at Chip as if he didn't believe him.

"I can show you if you want." Chip headed toward the old pen.

Mr. O'Dell followed him. "What about back there?" he asked, waving toward the woods.

"You can't go in there," Chip said. "It's too swampy in among the trees. You'd sink into the mud up to your belly button. It's, you know, water moccasin habitat. Once Luther and

65

I saw a deadly poisonous coral snake. That's why we stay away from there."

"I get the picture," Mr. O'Dell said. "Definitely too dangerous a place to take a bunch of schoolkids!" He laughed. "The way the school administration acts, you'd think I was risking my students' lives walking them a block down the street to observe lizards on a vacant lot." He looked around. "Where are these rabbits?"

"You have to be quiet," Chip said, as if Mr. O'Dell hadn't told the class that exact same thing five hundred times. "If you stay real still, they'll come out."

Mr. O'Dell checked for anthills, then settled down in the grass. Chip reached in his pocket for a handful of grain and made a line of it near Mr. O'Dell. Then he sat down next to him. They sat there very still and quiet.

One by one the rabbits came out of the bramble bushes and moved into the shorter grass in the pen. In fifteen minutes about twenty rabbits had appeared. Miz Rabbit, like always, hopped right up to Chip and got a handful of grain all to herself. Mr. O'Dell sat still as a statue—a statue with a very big grin—and didn't say a word. When the grain was all gone, the bunnies snuffled in the grass a few minutes, then hopped away.

"Some of them are white domestic rabbits," Mr. O'Dell observed. "Where did they come from?"

"The first one was white," Chip said. "Miz Rabbit. We set her free here." Chip didn't mention that he and Luther had rescued Miz Rabbit from a man who was keeping her locked in a dark garage. They'd never been caught, and Chip wasn't about to spill the beans now. "She's had lots of babies since. In fact," he added with a frown, "there used to be way more than this. Sometimes we've counted up to fifty."

"Maybe they're overrunning their food supply," Mr. O'Dell said. "That can happen if there aren't enough predators in the area."

Chip nodded, but he didn't think so. Although the rabbits kept the grass pretty short, there was plenty left.

The sun was about to dip below the horizon and he was beginning to feel chilled. His shorts were still wet from his hike through the swamp. He stood up and said, "I better be going."

Chip was surprised when Mr. O'Dell walked along next to him, pushing his bike along the dirt track. When they got to Lost Goat Lane, Mr. O'Dell stopped and looked back.

"That old place is pretty special to you, isn't it?" he asked.

Chip nodded.

"And you don't really want a bunch of people running all over the place and scaring off your rabbits, do you?"

The image of all the kids in his class stampeding around the Old Place made a lump form in Chip's throat. He shook his head and waited for Mr. O'Dell's next question. That was one thing you could count on from grown-ups. They always had a next question. But Mr. O'Dell didn't ask him anything else, at least, not right away. Instead, he told Chip something he didn't know.

"Most schools don't allow real field trips anymore. Oh, once or twice a year they might let the kids go to a theme park or something like that, but administrators don't even know the meaning of a *field* trip. And even if it was permitted, how much natural environment is there left around here?"

Mr. O'Dell let go of his bicycle handlebar with one hand and waved at the cornfields on both sides of Lost Goat Lane. "Farms and vacant lots—that's about as close as kids get to nature anymore, unless their parents take them to a state park or somewhere like that. But school trips where students can actually learn something about nature—forget it!" He shook his head sadly. "Small as this town is, I bet there aren't half a dozen kids in my class who have seen wild animals in their natural habitat."

They walked in silence for a while. Finally it was Chip, not Mr. O'Dell, who asked a question. "Reckon they would let you bring our class out to the Old Place?"

"Is that what you call it, 'the Old Place'?"

"Yes sir."

"If I could get permission, would it bother you too much? If we just came out one afternoon, for maybe an hour? And if I made everybody behave very respectfully, so they wouldn't scare the rabbits?"

They'd reached the place where the Martin driveway turned off Lost Goat Lane. Chip stopped and thought about what Mr. O'Dell had said. It was nice of him to ask, considering that the Old Place didn't belong to Chip or his family.

Chip knew that if Mr. O'Dell brought the class out, he would keep the kids from running wild. Mr. O'Dell didn't make his students walk in straight lines, two by two without talking, like some teachers did. But when they were in the field, he was good at keeping everybody fairly quiet and focused on what he thought was important.

"There's a ladder up to the loft in that old barn," Chip said finally. "You would want to move it, because if anybody climbed up there, they might fall through the floor, which is totally rotten."

"We would certainly want to do that," Mr. O'Dell agreed. "Any other risks you can think of?"

"They shouldn't swing on the railings of the old pen," Chip said. "Lily used to do that all the time, till one broke and she fell on her head."

"Good point." Mr. O'Dell laughed. "Anything else?"

"Nobody should go out in that bramble patch that used to be a pasture," Chip said. "And the woods behind that, they're *real* dangerous."

Mr. O'Dell looked at Chip for a minute. "I bet there's all kinds of wildlife back there," he said in a wistful voice.

"But *dangerous* wildlife. Ask Luther about the coral snake."

"I understand," Mr. O'Dell said. "Some places are better left alone. If a lot of people start tromping through, they're just not the same anymore, are they?"

"No sir," Chip said, kicking at the dirt with one mud-caked sneaker.

"So if we just stay there in the front part, around the old barn and where the house used to be, and act like serious field biologists, you think that would be acceptable?"

"I reckon the rabbits could live with that," Chip said, meaning that he figured he could live with it. There was something about the way Mr. O'Dell loved sharing what he knew about nature that made Chip want to share too.

Up to a point.

11

More Than Birds

The very next day, Mr. O'Dell announced that he had found a great place to visit and was in the process of getting approval from the principal to take the class there on a field trip.

Lily's hand shot up. "Where?" she asked.

"Out near where Chip lives." Mr. O'Dell was beaming. "It's an old abandoned farm."

"The Old Place?" Lily blurted out in astonishment.

"I think that's what Chip calls it," Mr. O'Dell said.

Chip cut his eyes sideways and saw Luther staring at him, lips pursed. Luther shook his head slowly from side to side in a way that said, clearer than words, *I can't believe you took him there. To our hideout! You traitor!*

Chip felt like screaming at him, *You don't even go there anymore! You're the traitor!* But of course he didn't say a word. To get away from Luther's stare, Chip went up to Mr. O'Dell's desk and asked him if he had a bird book he could borrow.

Mr. O'Dell said, "Why don't you use the Internet?"

"I want to look up a bird," Chip said, "but I don't know what kind it is."

"Oh. Then what you need is a good field guide to birds. Look on the shelf in the back of the classroom," Mr. O'Dell said.

Chip found a big guide to Florida birds and thumbed through the water bird section. He identified the white heron he had seen as a snowy egret. But he didn't know where to look for the big black bird. He carried the book up to Mr. O'Dell's desk. When Chip described the bird he was looking for, the teacher laughed. "Could it have been a buzzard?"

Chip laughed too. "No, it definitely wasn't a buzzard. This was a water bird. It swam with its whole body underwater."

"Black?" Mr. O'Dell mused. "Did you see it out of the water?"

"Yes," Chip said. "Black with some white on its back and wings."

"Could be an anhinga," Mr. O'Dell said, flipping through the pages of the bird book. "There? Is that it?"

Chip took the book from him and looked at the picture. "Yes sir," he said. "That's it, all right. It sat on a dead tree branch and spread its wings to dry just like that. An-hin-ga," he repeated, then looked up at his teacher. "Could I borrow this book for a while and take it home to read?"

"Well, I don't usually let students take out the reference books…"

Chip could tell that Mr. O'Dell really wanted to let him take the book, though, so he held onto it and waited.

Finally Mr. O'Dell said, "Why don't I just sign it out to you like a library book?" He scribbled the name of the book and the date on a note card. "Sign here and get it back to me in a week."

After school, Chip stopped at the house just long enough to grab a snack, a leftover piece of fried chicken from the fridge. Eating as he walked, he headed for the Jungle.

The Last Wild Place

When he got to the ditch—the one on the side with the biggest trees, not the one on the swampy side where it was harder to get across—he threw his pack across, then leapt over. This time he had a pretty good idea where the pond was, so it didn't take him long to get there. He found cat tracks in the mud again, plus some flattened-down patches of grass. He peered into the surrounding forest, but he didn't see any sign of a wild animal. He lay down in the grass, pulled the guidebook from his pack, and flipped through the pages. It was fun looking at the pictures, but after a while he lost interest. He put his head on his backpack and, without meaning to, drifted off to sleep.

Something brushing against his hand woke him up. He opened his eyes, his heart thumping like crazy. Crouched next to him was a cat, but not like any cat he'd ever seen. Chip knew instantly that it was a wildcat—not a grown one, but a kitten. It had a fuzzy kitten face, with a sort of black band that crossed over its nose and down each side of its mouth. There were little black lines above each eye, not horizontal like eyebrows, but straight up and down. It was like a first-grader had gotten hold of the kitten and made funny designs on its face fur with a black magic marker.

Chip lay absolutely still as the cat sniffed at his fingers. He watched it wobble down to the edge of the water and stand with its feet in the mud, right where he'd first seen the tracks. Chip lifted his head just enough to get a better look. The kitten started back up the bank toward him, loping along in that klutzy, unsteady way very young kittens have when they're just figuring out how much they can do. It saw him watching and stopped dead in its tracks. If Chip could have made his heart quit beating, he would have, just so he wouldn't scare it.

Suddenly Chip caught a movement out of the corner of his

eye, and his heart almost *did* stop. He turned his head quickly and there, bounding through the grass, was *another* klutzy kitten. Totally ignoring Chip, it made a big pouncing leap and landed on top of the first one. Over and over they rolled, gnawing at each other's furry necks and making growling noises.

Chip couldn't have said how long he watched them, whether it was two minutes or ten. They tumbled farther and farther away from him, but he didn't try to follow for fear of scaring them.

Then all of a sudden they both lifted their fuzzy little tails into the air and ran into the woods like they were being chased. *Or,* Chip thought, *maybe they've been called.* One thing was for sure, kittens that young weren't alone. Somewhere in those woods there was a mother wildcat.

Chip waited a little longer, then put the bird book in his backpack and left the Jungle. A million questions raced through his mind. The kittens hadn't seemed scared of him, so he imagined it might be easy to make friends with them. In fact, they'd hardly paid him any attention except when the first one had sniffed his fingers. Chip put his fingers to his nose. They smelled like the fried chicken he had eaten on his way to the Old Place.

He wondered if it would be dangerous to try to play with them. They could scratch and bite, but he didn't think they were big enough to hurt him. There was the mother to consider, though. What if she saw him try to pet her kittens and didn't like it? Where was she, anyway? Why hadn't he seen her? Had something happened to her? Were they orphans?

Should he take them something to eat? He'd have to figure out a way to find out what kind of cats they were without asking Mr. O'Dell for a book on wildcats. He didn't want him to get curious.

By the time Chip got to Lost Goat Lane, he felt dizzy from all the questions going around in his head. He desperately wanted to tell someone what he'd just seen, but there was really only one person he could trust with a secret this precious. And that was Luther. Chip whirled around and headed toward the Wilsons', running as fast as he could.

Ruby was sitting on the porch swing talking on the new cell phone Mr. Jackson had given her for Christmas. When Chip came bounding up onto the porch, she moved the phone away from her mouth and said, "Luther's in his room, but I don't know if—"

"Thanks!" Chip said, and dashed into the house and down the hall to Luther's room.

Luther was sitting on the floor with a music book open beside him and a flute in his hand. Chip dropped to his knees facing him. "Luther, come with me! I've got to show you something!"

Luther frowned. "Come where?"

"To the Old Place."

"Why don't you show your friend Mr. O'Dell?" Luther looked back down at the music book and started tootling on the flute like Chip wasn't even there.

"Luther!" Chip put all the urgency he could in his voice. "Please! This is something we don't want *any*body to find out!"

Luther looked back at Chip. As their eyes met, something told Chip that even though Luther was acting cold, he was glad Chip had come. Without speaking, Luther put down the flute, then kicked off his soccer shoes and stepped into his sneakers.

Chip dropped his backpack on Luther's bed. "I'll come back for this later," he said. "We've got to hurry."

As they passed through the living room, Mrs. Wilson called, "Luther, supper's going to ready soon, so you boys don't be gone long, hear?" Chip knew she was smiling because she thought everything was okay with him and Luther again. Things weren't entirely okay yet, but he hoped they would be once Luther saw what he had to show him.

Chip figured they didn't have more than an hour of daylight left, so he started off at a trot.

Luther lagged behind. "What is it you want to show me?" he called.

"You'll see," Chip said, and hoped it was true. He didn't know how Luther would react if they got to the Jungle and the kittens weren't there. After all, Chip had been there three times before he'd seen them.

"Tell me!" Luther demanded, slowing down to a walk.

"I can't."

Luther came to a full stop on the road. "Why not?"

By then Chip was a little way ahead of him. He turned around and came back. "Because," he said, "you wouldn't believe me."

Luther looked embarrassed. Maybe he remembered how he'd practically called Chip a liar when he told him about Booker and Mom kissing. Or maybe he didn't. But it didn't really matter. What mattered was that he started walking again, and when Chip started jogging, Luther jogged along beside him.

When Chip veered off into the cornfield, Luther stopped again. "I thought we were going to the Old Place."

"We are," Chip said over his shoulder. "The back part."

"The *Jungle?*"

Chip kept moving because he could hear the swish of corn leaves letting him know that Luther was right behind him. When they got to the place where it was easiest to jump the ditch, Chip made a flying leap and landed safely on the other side. Luther hesitated a split second, then came sailing across the ditch and hit the ground next to him on all fours.

Luther stood up, eyeing the tangled undergrowth. "I don't see a trail."

"There's no trail. But I know the way," Chip assured him.

They pushed through the ragweed and into the forest where the brush thinned out and it was easier walking. The forest floor was in shadow, but the sun still glinted through the treetops, so there was plenty of light. Chip led the way along the route he had used before. As they approached the open area where the knoll and the marshy pond were, Chip held his fingers to his lips. He moved forward in slow, silent steps. Luther followed right on his heels. When there was only a thin screen of bushes between them and the grassy area, Chip stopped so Luther could take it in. The edges near the forest were dark, but the middle was still in sunshine.

"Holy cow!" Luther breathed. "What's *that?*"

He pointed at the anhinga, sitting on the dead tree stump with its wings spread, catching the last rays of the sun. It probably wasn't more than ten feet from them, and it had a wingspread of least three feet.

"Anhinga," Chip whispered, and again put a finger to his lips. He dropped to his knees and crawled almost to the edge of the grassy knoll. "There's more," he whispered to Luther. "If we didn't scare them away."

As they lay on their bellies in the grass, Chip was impressed by how motionless Luther stayed, especially since it was near sunset and mosquitoes were beginning to come out in droves. In fact, the bugs were so bad that Chip was just about to give up and say they'd have to come back another day when his eye caught a movement at the far side of the knoll. He held his breath.

He didn't think Luther saw it at first. In fact, he wasn't even sure he'd seen anything. Then there it was: a kitten face that disappeared when another kitten leapt on it from behind. They tumbled end over end, out of the forest and into a spot of sunlit grass.

Luther sucked wind, gripping Chip's arm tight enough to dent his biceps.

The whole show only lasted a minute, then the kittens scurried back into the bushes. When the last flicker of sunlight left the knoll, Chip figured they'd better get out of there before the mosquitoes carried them off. He motioned to Luther and, still on their knees, they backed up into the trees before standing. They walked back the way they had come, neither saying a word.

They were all the way out on the road when Luther turned to Chip and exclaimed, "Those weren't regular cats!"

"I know," Chip agreed. "What kind do you think they are?"

"Panthers, maybe?"

Chip shook his head. "I've seen Florida panthers in the Palm Beach Zoo. They're light brown all over. These kittens are spotted, and they have funny marks on their faces."

"Did you see any panther babies at the zoo?"

"No," Chip admitted, heading toward the Wilsons' place.

"Some baby animals are a different color from the adults," Luther suggested. "For camouflage, so the mother can hide them better."

"Could be," Chip agreed. "I don't know if these kittens have a mother. I've never seen her. Or any big tracks either."

"They're pretty young to be on their own," Luther pointed out. "I mean, to be catching their own food."

"True."

"Who else knows about them?" Luther asked.

Chip looked at him in surprise. "Nobody. Why?"

"You didn't tell O'Dell?"

"Course not! Why would I tell him?"

"You told him about the Old Place."

"No, I didn't. He found it on his own. I was back in the Jungle and didn't even know he was there until I walked by the old barn and heard him hollering."

"What was he hollering about?"

Chip grinned. "He had ants in his pants. Real ones."

Luther snickered.

Chip started hopping around, pretending to be Mr. O'Dell. He yelped and whooped and slapped at his legs until they were both laughing like crazy.

They suddenly stopped laughing, seeming to have serious thoughts at the same time. "We have to keep this a secret," Chip said.

"How can we, when O'Dell's already planning a field trip out here?"

"I told him it was dangerous back there, all swampy and full of snakes. It seemed like that scared him off. He promised to keep the kids in the area up front, around the old barn and the place where the cow pen used to be."

By the time they got to the Wilsons' yard, it was getting

dark. Chip could hear people talking in the kitchen and the clink of silverware. Luther was late for supper. Chip went into the house with Luther to get his backpack.

"Is that our boys coming home after dark?" Mrs. Wilson called out.

"Our boys or burglars," Mr. Wilson said loudly, with a chuckle in his voice.

"Sorry I'm late, Grandma," Luther said.

"It was my fault," Chip said.

Ruby smiled at Chip. "Looks like you're going to be even later getting home to your supper. How about I call your mom and see if you can stay and have leftovers with Luther?"

Chip looked at Luther.

"Yeah." Luther grinned and shoved his plate over so Ruby could put another one beside it. Chip slid into the chair next to him.

12
Field Trip

When the bus arrived at their stop Tuesday morning, Chip and Luther got on together the way they used to and slid into the same seat, just in front of Lily.

Lily leaned forward. "Chip, why don't you come to the community center today?"

"Can't," Chip said.

"Me either," Luther said.

"What's going on?" Lily demanded. "First you don't want to play because you're mad at each other, and now you don't want to play because you're friends again!" She thumped Chip on the shoulder. "Come on, Chip! You were *good* on defense. If you practiced, you'd be awesome!"

Chip shrugged his thumped shoulder and didn't look at her. She turned to Luther. "What about you, Luther? You know those guys at the center depend on you. And not just in soccer. They think you're their *friend*."

"I am their friend," Luther mumbled.

"Not if you drop them like *that!*" Lily snapped her fingers under Luther's nose. Then she sat back in her seat, looking like a small thundercloud.

Luther stared at the seat in front of him for a minute, then looked back at Lily. "I'll come to practice tomorrow. And some other days. But not *every* day."

"Me too," Chip said. He didn't want to give up even one minute in the Jungle, but if they hurried home on the days they played soccer and went straight to the Old Place, they'd still have a little time to spend there before dark. And they could stay all day on Saturdays and Sundays.

Luther glanced over at Chip with a small smile. Chip could tell they were both thinking more or less the same thing. It was just like old times.

Naturally Lily wasn't completely satisfied with that plan, but she quit bugging them. Chip knew that someday he'd have to explain to her how he and Luther wanted to do more than just play sports.

But they weren't ready to share their secret yet.

After lunch, Mr. O'Dell announced that the field trip was scheduled for Thursday afternoon. As he was handing out permission slips, somebody asked what they should wear. Chip was glad when Mr. O'Dell told them shorts would be fine, because even the wildest kids wouldn't try to cross the thorny-bushed pasture with bare legs. The Jungle would be as safe from them as it had been from Chip and Luther and everyone else who had used the Old Place as a hideout through the years.

Chip and Luther went with Lily to the community center after school on Wednesday. Soccer practice ran longer than usual, and it was late when they started walking home. Luther and Chip didn't get a chance to talk about the Jungle until they left Lily at the nursery. They headed down Lost Goat Lane at a trot, but by the time they reached the Old Place the sun was already dipping behind the cornstalks. In another few minutes it would be out of sight altogether.

Then Chip remembered something. He had promised Mr. O'Dell that he'd move the ladder leading to the loft so nobody would climb up there during the field trip and get hurt. He and Luther hoisted the old ladder between them and stuck it in a dark corner of the barn where it wouldn't be noticed.

By the time they'd finished, the sun had set. "I think it's too late," Luther said.

Chip nodded. "We barely had time to see anything before, it got dark so quick. Tomorrow we'll come earlier and—"

"Tomorrow's Thursday," Luther reminded him. "Field trip day."

"Oh yeah. But there won't be any need for us to ride the bus back to school. After they all leave, we'll stay here and get an early start into the Jungle."

"Yeah!" Luther said excitedly. "That's what we'll do!"

But that was not what they did, because on Thursday, something unexpected happened while they were at the Old Place.

Even though it wasn't as exciting as going to an amusement park, everybody was happy to be going on a real field trip. Mr. O'Dell had emphasized that this trip was for the purposes of scientific observation, and he explained how he wanted every student to observe and take notes on something. Their homework for the weekend would be writing up their field notes, to be turned in on Monday. This, he'd said, was in preparation for a longer research report that would include not only what they personally had observed, but also information on the topic from books and magazines and reliable websites.

Mr. O'Dell first led the students around the foundation of the old house to look at lizards and ants and spiderwebs, pretty much the same stuff they might see on any vacant lot. Near panic broke out when somebody sighted a gopher snake. But once it was identified as nonpoisonous, several kids took notes until the snake got tired of being observed and slid away under a pile of rubble. Somebody found a bird's nest in one of the hibiscus bushes, and that drew a small crowd of note-takers for a few minutes. Next the teacher led the kids into the barn and showed them how to look through the droppings from the owl's nest. The discovery of three rat skulls generated a lot of interest, plus a squabble over who saw them first and should get to keep them. Then it was time for the rabbit show.

Mr. O'Dell instructed the students to sit down in the grass and be very quiet. Everyone did as they were told, because they had long ago learned that Mr. O'Dell only asked them to be quiet when he had something interesting to share with them. Chip and Luther made a row of grain across the pen in front of the kids. Then they all waited. The first to emerge from the brambles was Miz Rabbit. She ignored the grain and hopped right up to Lily, who gave her some corn chips from her pocket. A few more white rabbits came out, followed by a mother swamp rabbit and her five little ones.

When the baby rabbits appeared, the class made a low *ooohh* sound, and a couple of the rabbits skittered back into the bushes. The others stayed until every last bit of grain was gone. The students were so entranced that some of them completely forgot to make notes.

Chip, Luther, and Lily silently counted the rabbits and exchanged worried glances. Why only seventeen rabbits, when a month ago they'd counted more than fifty?

When the rabbits had finished the grain and hopped back into the bushes, Mr. O'Dell blew his whistle to signal that it was time to go. The two parents who had come along as chaperones started herding everyone toward the bus. Just then, a silver pickup drove up and three men got out. Without saying a word to anyone in the school group, they began tromping around the Old Place, pointing and talking.

Chip and Luther hung back, hoping to hear what the men were saying. The two boys had given Mr. O'Dell notes from their mothers saying they could be left at the Old Place, but the principal hadn't allowed it. She told Mr. O'Dell that everyone had to be brought back to school so they could take the regular school bus home, which made perfect sense to the principal, but no sense at all to Chip and Luther.

"Come on, boys," Mr. O'Dell called. "Time to go."

Just as Chip turned to get on the bus, he heard something that scared the daylights out of him.

"How far back does it go?" one of the workers asked.

Chip froze.

"All the way to the back of those trees yonder," said the other man.

"Nice parcel," the first man said. "What a deal!"

Mr. O'Dell took a couple of steps toward the group of men. "Hello," he said, putting out his hand. "I'm Mark O'Dell, a teacher at the grade school. Just brought my class out for a little nature study."

A man with biceps almost as big as Chip's thighs shook Mr. O'Dell's hand and said, "Bob Blake, developer."

"You own this place?" Mr. O'Dell asked.

Chip thought that was a strange question, because he'd already told Mr. O'Dell that it belonged to the Franklin family.

"Leased it," Mr. Blake said.

"What're you planning to build?" Mr. O'Dell asked. "I would've thought that land way out here, no paved roads or anything, wouldn't be good for much besides farming."

"It'll work fine for a meatpacking plant," Mr. Blake said. "You ever smelled one of them places? The farther out the better."

"Wow!" Mr. O'Dell said, sounding like he was really impressed. "I didn't realize you were a major developer. But isn't that a big investment to put on leased property?"

"Normally, yeah," Mr. Blake agreed. "Not in this case, though. The owner's an old lady. She has a sentimental attachment to the property and flat refuses to sell. But when I told her how it was all grown up in weeds, she agreed to lease me the front half, providing I cleaned it up." Bob Blake chuckled. "I'll clean it up, all right. There won't be a blade of grass left standing, let alone that mess." He waved contemptuously toward the old barn.

"What about the back, where the trees are?" Chip called, speaking up for the first time.

"We'll leave it for now," Blake said. "But the old lady's in a nursing home. She won't live much longer. When she kicks off, the property will go to the estate, and they'll sell it for way under market value." He grinned at Mr. O'Dell. "And I mean *way* under. Because who's going to want land next to a meatpacking plant?"

While Bob Blake was talking, the other two men had stretched out a long tape and were taking measurements. Mr.

O'Dell put one hand on Chip's shoulder and the other on Luther's. "Come on, boys," he said. "We've got to get back to school. Mr. Blake and his men have work to do."

Chip broke away from Mr. O'Dell and ran to the bus. Luther, looking as torn up as Chip felt, followed with their teacher. Mr. O'Dell didn't look too good either. He just slouched down in the front seat behind the driver and said, "Let's go, Johnny. No point in sitting here while the developers of the world pave over another piece of paradise."

As soon as they got back to school, Lily and Ruben started in on Chip and Luther about coming to play soccer.

"Okay," Luther said, trying to act interested.

Chip said okay too, because he didn't want to let the community center kids down either. But once they started playing, Chip couldn't keep his mind on the game. Twice he let a player from the other team steal the ball from him.

"See?" Lily had shouted at him. "That's what happens when you don't practice every day!"

Luther must have realized how upset Chip was, because after Lily turned off at the nursery, he said something right out of the blue that made Chip feel better. "You know when you told me about Booker and your mom?" he asked.

"Yeah?" Chip said cautiously.

"I didn't really think you were lying. I was just...you know...not liking the idea of more changes."

Chip didn't say anything, mainly because he was afraid that if he said the wrong thing it might make Luther mad again.

After a minute, Luther asked, "Do you think they're *serious*? Like they really might get married?"

Chip wanted to avoid answering, but if he didn't say anything, that would only make Luther suspicious. He figured that the best way to keep Luther's trust was to just tell him the truth. "I don't know," he said. "The night after I saw them kissing, Booker came by. Nobody was there to help him get his wheelchair in the house, so Mom went out to talk to him in the van. I could see them from my window, and I didn't see any more kissing. They were just talking."

"Oh," Luther said. "How about since then?"

"Well, they do talk on the phone a lot," Chip admitted.

"What about?"

"Silly stuff. Booker says things to Mom that make her laugh, and then she tells him funny stories about customers at the nursery."

"Like what?" Luther quizzed.

"Well, like this woman who said all the neighborhood dogs came to pee in her yard. She wanted to buy some kind of shrub that dogs especially like, so they'd all pee in that one place instead of on all her other plants."

Luther began to giggle. "So what did Mr. Hashimoto sell her?"

Chip laughed too. "I don't know. Maybe sweet *pea* vines?"

"Sweet pea vines for dogs to pee on. Oh man," he groaned, "that has to be the worst joke you've come up with yet!"

When Luther said that, Chip knew for sure that things were back to normal between them. Whatever Mom and Booker decided to do about getting married, he didn't think Luther would blame him. It was a good feeling to know they were on the same side again.

At supper, Chip told Mom and Kate what the developer had told Mr. O'Dell.

"Peee-yew!" Kate yelped. "We don't want a meatpacking plant just down the road! Mom, can't you do something?"

"Good grief!" Mom exclaimed. "If they put a meatpacking plant out here, next thing they'd want a slaughterhouse. Maybe even a feedlot! If they started running cattle trucks in and out along Lost Goat Lane, this place wouldn't be fit to live in!"

"Wouldn't need a meatpacking plant if everybody was a vegetarian," Chip muttered, deciding right then and there that as soon as he finished the meatloaf he was eating, he was going become a vegetarian like Luther.

"That'll never happen," Kate said.

"No," Mom agreed. "But there must be something we can do. Monday I'll check on the zoning laws."

13

A Rainy Friday

Around noon on Friday it started raining. It was still pouring when Lily, Chip, and Luther got off the school bus that afternoon.

"Wanna stay overnight?" Chip asked Luther as soon as Lily veered off to the nursery. "If it stops raining, we can go to the Old Place early in the morning."

"Yeah!" Luther said.

"Okay," Chip said. "When we get to my house, I'll call the nursery and ask Mom."

Mom said it was all right for Luther to spend the night if it was okay with Ruby. When Luther called his mother, she said yes, but she insisted that he come home first to get a change of clothes and his toothbrush.

The rain had let up a little, so Chip and Luther put their rain jackets back on and set out for the Wilsons' house. By the time they got to the dirt track that led to the Old Place, the rain was falling in torrents. A silver pickup was parked near the old barn.

"That's Mr. Blake's truck!" Chip exclaimed. Without another word, he and Luther turned toward the Old Place.

When Chip and Luther walked up to the truck, Mr. Blake was still inside, talking on a cell phone. He pushed the off button and opened the window a crack. "Hi, kids. What brings you out in weather like this?"

"Just coming from school, sir," Luther said politely. "We live on Lost Goat Lane."

"We saw your truck and came to see what was going on," Chip added. "Where are your men?"

"They'll be here on Monday to run a survey line," Blake said. "I'll do the grading on Tuesday."

At first Chip didn't understand what Mr. Blake meant by *grading*. It sounded like he was planning to grade his men on how hard they worked. Then Chip realized that he'd been thinking of the wrong kind of grading.

"This is pretty low-lying land." Mr. Blake lit a cigarette and gestured toward the Old Place. "I came out here this afternoon to see how swampy it gets when it's raining. A dozer can get stuck if the ground's too soggy."

"You mean a bulldozer?" Chip asked.

Mr. Blake laughed. "Yeah. I could push that old barn down by leaning against it. But I'll let the dozer do it. Barn, bushes, house foundations—they'll all be graded flat as a pancake by this time next week."

"There's an owl's nest in the barn," Luther said in a small voice.

"I wouldn't be surprised. You usually find them in places like this." Mr. Blake chuckled. "That old owl had better hope her younguns can fly by Tuesday, because that's when I reckon it's gonna come down."

"Couldn't you leave the barn standing? Fix it up and use it for storage or something?" Chip suggested.

Mr. Blake started his truck engine. "No need. My plant's going to cover this entire area." He waved his arm in an arc that included everything from the foundations where the house had been to the bramble-covered pasture. "Come back next Friday," he invited cheerfully. "You boys won't recognize this place. Want a ride home?"

"No thanks," Luther said.

"See you next week then." Mr. Blake rolled up his window and drove away.

Chip and Luther tromped back to Lost Goat Lane, the hoods of their rain jackets pulled up. "Wish *he'd* get stuck in the mud," Luther muttered. "He doesn't even care that the barn owls will get killed when they tear down the barn."

"Everybody's like that," Chip said sadly. "You know how it is when they burn the cane fields or plow up the cornstalks. Swamp rabbits scatter in every direction and birds fly, but only a few get out. All the babies get left behind—burnt up or plowed under—and nobody even cares."

"Yeah, but this is even worse," Luther said. "That old lady who owns this land *does* care. Remember what Blake said yesterday? He said she leased it to him because he told her he'd clean the place up!"

Chip nodded. "There's another way this is worse. Cornfields get plowed up every year, so not that many animals live there to start with. But the Old Place hasn't been disturbed for years and years. That back part might be like the Everglades was thousands of years ago. I bet we haven't seen a fraction of the wildlife that lives back there."

They slogged on in silence, the rain pouring down.

They shed their rain jackets and wet sneakers out on the porch. Inside, Mrs. Wilson was sitting on the sofa weaving strips of fabric into a rag rug, like the ones on the floor.

Ruby was at the desk, writing something in a notebook. "You boys look like drowned rats!" she exclaimed. "Luther, get in there and get some dry clothes on. Chip, you want to borrow some dry jeans?"

"I'm okay," Chip said. "I'll wait till I get home." He didn't see any point in changing since he was just going to get wet again when they walked back to his house.

Mrs. Wilson laid aside her handiwork and got up from the sofa. "I bet if I offered you boys some hot chocolate, you'd turn me down flat."

"No, ma'am," Chip said, following her into the kitchen.

Mrs. Wilson poured milk into a pot and set it on the stove to heat. "Luther told us about that builder you all met over at the Old Place," she said. "That just breaks my heart."

"We saw him there again today," Chip told her. "He says that by the end of next week, he'll have the whole front part graded flat as a pancake."

"Oh my!" Mrs. Wilson took a can of cocoa out of the cupboard and began measuring it into the milk. "If Mrs. Franklin knew what he was doing to her place, she'd probably get up out of that nursing home and come whack him on the head with a stick."

"Do you know Mrs. Franklin?" Chip asked.

"I did," Mrs. Wilson said. "The Franklins lived over there when I was a little girl. That honeysuckle and hibiscus and crepe myrtle, Mrs. Franklin planted every bit of it. And all kinds of fruit trees. Lots of them didn't take in this wet climate, and I reckon the ones that did died off over the years. But I tell you, in her day that place was a true paradise."

"So you were like…friends?" Chip asked.

"Well, yes, in a manner of speaking. But that was an awful long time ago," Mrs. Wilson said as she measured out sugar and added it to the cocoa. "After the house burned down and they moved away, we exchanged Christmas cards for I don't know how many years. Then her husband died, and after a while the cards stopped coming. I haven't heard from her in a real long time. She was up in Atlanta then, but I don't have any idea where she is now."

Mrs. Wilson turned to smile at Chip. "Wherever she is, I sure hope there's lots of flowers and trees. I never saw a woman who loved nature like she did."

"What about the back part?" Chip asked. "Did she plant that too?'

"Out past the pasture, you mean?" Mrs. Wilson cocked her head, trying to remember. "One time she brought a couple of coconut palms from the coast and put them back there, but that's all I can recall."

Mrs. Wilson looked up and smiled as Luther walked in with his backpack. "Mrs. Franklin had a notion that folks ought not cultivate every inch of their land. She said that some part of everybody's property should be left natural for the wildlife. I guess her husband agreed with her, because he left that swampy part just the way nature made it."

"How come Grandpa didn't do that here?" Luther asked.

"This place was already farmed down to the last inch when we bought it," Mrs. Wilson explained. "Except for that strip of saw grass along the drainage ditch there on the back side."

She stirred the cocoa round and round in the pot, smiling the way people do when they're remembering something from long ago that makes them feel good. "I never forgot what Mrs. Franklin said about the wildlife needing a place to live too. So years later, when Sam and I bought this place, I said, 'Sam, you just leave that saw grass back there for the birds and small critters to make their nests in.' He did, and I do believe he lets it grow an inch or two wider every year. Of course, it's nothing like the woods on the back side of the Old Place. Mrs. Franklin used to call it her private little Everglades."

"That's a good name for it," Chip said. "But now even the Everglades is getting wrecked."

"It's true that a lot of the Glades has been drained for farm-ing and housing developments," she said. "But there's a bunch of good folks working hard to save what's left."

"Yeah," Luther said under his breath to Chip, "but we're not a bunch of folks."

They sat down at the kitchen table and Mrs. Wilson put a cup of steaming cocoa in front of each of them. "Hot!" Mrs. Wilson warned. "Give it a minute, and test it before you take a sip. I don't want you burning your tongues."

"Yes ma'am." Chip stared at the cocoa, but he was thinking about where they might find a bunch of good folks who'd help them save the Old Place.

14

One More in the Jungle

Saturday morning the sky was clear. As soon as they'd had breakfast, milked the goats, and fed the ducks, Chip and Luther left for the Jungle. This time Chip took Luther in from the marshy side. They waded in water up past their knees and got sopping wet. When they got to the knoll, they took off their sneakers and jeans, put them in the sun to dry, and settled down to watch the pond.

Luther had never seen the anhinga swimming like Chip had, so he didn't realize it was the same bird until it hopped up on the dead tree branch and spread its wings. After about an hour the snowy white egret appeared, and moments later a second one landed beside it. The two tall birds waded around the marshy pond, spearing whatever they could find in the water. When the egrets flew off, Chip and Luther crawled over to the edge of the pond and lay on their bellies. Beneath the surface they could see crawdads and some tiny fish.

They had been lying like that for a long time, with their arms folded in the mud and their noses practically touching the water, when Chip saw Luther turn his head slowly to the side, like he was trying to see something behind them. In the same instant, something tickled the bottom of one of Chip's feet. He jerked his head around, and the sudden movement spooked the two wild kittens. He and Luther barely glimpsed their behinds as they went skittering back into the bushes.

"Rats!" Luther said under his breath. "I still didn't get a good look at them."

They stayed still a very long time after that, hoping the kittens would come back. This time they lay facing the forest, and listened hard.

When they finally did hear something, it was definitely *not* a kitten. From the amount of noise it had to be a very large animal thrashing through the underbrush. *Should we lie still?* Chip wondered. *Climb a tree? Or run like crazy?*

Then a voice called, "Luther? Chip? Where *are* you?"

"Lily!" Luther exclaimed, and both boys began to giggle with relief.

Chip called, "Over here!"

A minute later Lily came bursting out of the bushes. She was wearing shorts, as usual, and was scratched all over.

"How'd you find us?" Chip asked.

"I saw your tracks in the mud, where you turned off the road into the cornfield. I just followed your trail. If you can call that a trail!" She went over to the edge of the pond and scooped up a handful water to wash off the blood that was dribbling down her arm from a nasty scratch.

"You shouldn't have worn shorts," Luther said.

"Sorry." Lily grinned. "I didn't know the dress code for back here was boy's underwear."

That set Chip and Luther to giggling again, and also reminded them that they should put on their jeans, which they did.

Lily looked around, taking in the grassy knoll, the marshy pond, and the trees hung with Spanish moss. "This is a fantastic place," she said. "How long have you known about it?"

"A week," Chip said.

"Thanks for telling me!"

"I didn't think you'd be interested." Chip waved his arm around the knoll. "After all, it's not big enough to play soccer in here."

"Chip," Lily said, "*any*place is big enough to practice. If you don't believe it, ask my mom. She confiscated my soccer ball for a day when she caught me practicing in the hall."

"This is no place to practice either," Luther said quietly. "There's a lot of stuff to see if you stay still."

Lily lowered her voice. "Like what?"

Chip could tell she was beginning to get the feel of the place. "Two snowy white egrets," he told her. "And some crawdads."

"Plus a big black anhinga," Luther added. He looked at Chip, his eyes asking a question.

Lily saw the look and asked, "What else?"

Chip realized that Luther was probably thinking that since he had discovered the place, it was up to him to decide whether to tell her or not.

"Might as well," Chip said to Luther.

"Might as well," Luther repeated.

Lily looked from one boy to the other. The blood was trickling down her arm again, but she ignored it. "This is something big, isn't it?"

"Not big," Chip said. "But special. Just about the most special thing I've ever laid eyes on."

"Me too," Luther said.

"What?" Lily asked.

"Kittens. Florida panthers."

"You're *kidding!*"

"He's not kidding," Luther said. "It's just that we're not sure they're panthers, because we haven't had a good look yet. At least, I haven't."

"Did you see that Discovery Channel program about Florida panthers?" Lily asked excitedly. "The baby panthers looked different from the grown ones. Did the kittens you saw have black spots and a funny black moustache across their nose and two white triangles right here?" She drew triangles on her upper lip and on either side of her nose.

Chip nodded. That was *exactly* the way he remembered the kitten face.

"Oh my gosh!" Lily breathed. "This is even *better* than soccer. This is like *magic*."

"Better than magic," Luther said. "Because it's *real*."

"I wish it was magic," Chip said. "Because then we could find a way to keep those builder guys from wiping this place out."

Lily's puzzled expression reminded Chip that she didn't know anything about the developer. She was already on the bus when Mr. Blake explained his plan to Mr. O'Dell, and Chip and Luther hadn't had a chance to tell her about it.

"You know those guys who showed up the day of our field trip?" Luther said. "We heard the boss tell Mr. O'Dell that he was going to bulldoze the barn and the meadow and build a meatpacking plant there. They can't do anything with this part of the property right now, but when the owner dies..." Luther's voice trailed off.

Chip picked a blade of grass and began to tear it into small strips. "Mom thinks that once he has the meatpacking plant, he might want to put a slaughterhouse and a feedlot back here."

"Holy smoke!" Lily exclaimed. "You can smell those feedlots for miles! My dad is going to flip out when he hears about this!"

"The whole idea makes me sick," Chip said. "Even if they just clear the front part, that's where the rabbits live. They've got burrows all over the old pasture, in among the bramble bushes."

Just then the big anhinga flapped down onto the pond, plunged its head in the water, and came up with a small fish speared on its beak. Lily gasped. "That was *amazing!*" Then she asked, "When do I get to see the baby panthers?"

"It takes a long time," Chip told her. "At least an hour."

Lily glanced up at her watch. "I don't have an hour. We've got a game at the community center this afternoon. That's why I came looking for you guys."

Luther shook his head. "I already told you I don't want to play soccer every day."

"You didn't play yesterday," Lily reminded him.

"We played Wednesday and Thursday," Chip said.

"Yeah," Lily countered, "but on Thursday you played really lousy. If you want to be good, you have to practice more." She looked at Luther. "Besides, those kids are *your* friends. More than mine anyway. There's not much for them to do on the weekend."

Chip could tell Luther didn't want to leave the Jungle any more than he did, but he felt guilty about copping out on the community center kids.

"Come on," Lily wheedled. "I have to get home, but you can stay awhile longer. Stop by my house after lunch and we'll go together. Please? The game will only take a couple of hours. You'd still have time to come back down here afterwards."

"Oh, all right," Luther said reluctantly.

After the game that afternoon, Chip, Luther, and Lily walked home together. Lily was in a good mood because Chip and Luther had come, and Luther was in a good mood because he had played well. Chip thought it was a good time to bring up something he'd been thinking about ever since Mrs. Wilson mentioned that there was a bunch of good people working to save the Everglades.

"We should to try to save the Old Place," Chip said.

Luther snorted. "Not a chance. Adults can keep kids from doing what they want, plus they can make them do things they don't want to do." He kicked at an empty soda can on the path like he was mad at it, and added, "But we can't stop *them* from doing whatever they please—like making you move when you don't want to."

"Old man Grimsted didn't get away with mistreating Little Billy and Miz Rabbit," Chip reminded him. "We put a stop to that."

"True," Luther admitted. "But I don't see how we can save the Old Place. Only grown-ups could do that, if they even cared."

"My parents care," Lily said. "When I told them about the meatpacking plant, my dad said it would ruin his business. I asked how, and my mom said because you can't sell people roses when all they can smell is dead cattle. Or whatever kind of meat they're going to pack there."

"My mom cares too," Chip said. "She's going to check with the zoning people to see if it's legal to build a meatpacking plant out there."

"If that guy doesn't have all the right permits, my dad thinks he can be stopped," Lily put in.

"Yeah," Luther said. "But what if he does?"

No one had an answer for that. They walked in silence for a while. Chip's thoughts jumped all over the place. As soon as he'd get an idea, he'd see that it wouldn't work. He kept coming back to the main problem. "There's not enough of us," he said. "We need a bunch of people."

"Yeah," Lily said. "Like those environmentalists who block roads to stop loggers from cutting down old-growth forests. Or Greenpeace people who put themselves between whale boats and whales so the hunters can't harpoon them."

"Some protests are illegal," Luther reminded her.

Chip shrugged. "So was what we did to save Little Billy and Miz Rabbit."

"Yeah, but we were just little kids. If we'd gotten caught, they wouldn't really have sent us to jail. We just thought they would," Luther recalled. "Anyway, that's not the point. The point is that nobody's going to pay any mind to three sixth-grade protesters. If we got in front of Mr. Blake's bulldozer, he'd probably squash us flat."

"No way!" Lily punched the air with her fist. "If he did, my dad would squash *him* flat." She grinned. "Unless your moms got there at the same time. Then they'd probably get in a fight over who got to roll over Blake first."

Luther laughed, but Chip didn't. "Lily, do you honestly think we could go out there and stop Mr. Blake?"

Lily hesitated. "Well, no. Not by ourselves."

"Who else is there?" Luther asked.

"What about the community center kids? Maybe they'd come one afternoon and we could do a sit-down strike or something."

Luther frowned. "Why would they care?"

"Well, Jesse and Kishan and Ralph are in our class and went on the field trip. They *might* care," Lily said, but she didn't sound all that certain.

"What about the rest of the class?" Chip asked, for the first time feeling a tiny bit hopeful. "And Mr. O'Dell. He *loves* the Old Place."

"I'll ask the class to help if you'll ask Mr. O'Dell. After all," Lily teased, "you're the teacher's pet." She turned to Luther.

"You should ask the kids at the center. At least the ones we play soccer with."

"Why don't you ask them? You're the one who runs the soccer games."

"Because, Luther, you're the one who first made friends with them, when everybody else was ignoring them. They *like* you."

"All right, I'll ask," Luther said. "But don't blame me if they say no."

"Even if Mr. O'Dell and the class and all the community center kids say yes," Chip said, "we still have a problem."

"What?" Luther and Lily asked together.

"Mr. Blake is going to bring the bulldozer first thing Tuesday morning. So we'd have to ditch class. If we head for the Old Place instead of getting on the school bus, our moms aren't going to squash Mr. Blake; they'll squash *us*."

15
Family Matters

On Friday Lily had told her father that she'd help out at the nursery when she got home from school, so she couldn't go to the Jungle with Chip and Luther. She made them promise to wait for her in the morning so she could go with them then.

Chip and Luther were about to cross the highway to Lost Goat Lane when Luther's grandfather, who worked at the nursery, called from the parking lot, "Hey, there! How'd you boys like to help me carry some plants to the house?"

Chip and Luther looked at each other. They wouldn't have minded helping Mr. Wilson, but they were in a hurry to get to the Jungle. If they didn't go right then, it would soon be too dark to go at all.

Mr. Wilson saw the look and asked, "You boys got some other plans?"

"No sir." Chip would rather have told him the truth, but the problem with telling grown-ups the truth was that you usually couldn't tell one part of it—they always wanted the whole story. And since he and Luther didn't want the grown-ups to know about the Jungle, the best thing to do was to forget about going that afternoon.

"Where's the stuff you want us to carry, Grandpa?" Luther asked.

"Over here on this table," Mr. Wilson replied, leading them back through the nursery. "These wilted tomato plants and this hanging basket that's done blooming. Mr. Hashimoto was going to throw them out, but I asked him if my Sarah could have them." He winked at the boys. "No plant in her care would dare to get wilty."

Chip and Luther slung their backpacks over their shoulders, and each of them picked up a couple of plant containers. Mr. Wilson carried the hanging basket and together they crossed the highway. Luther's grandfather was strong, but slow. He often said that he and Old Billy were growing old together, and if he grew a beard like the goat's, people probably couldn't tell them apart. Chip and Luther walked on either side of him, and he told them about what it was like back in the old days, when the area was all small farms.

"One by one the small farmers along the Lane sold out to the big farmers, all except us and the family that owned the place where you live, Chip. Your folks got that."

Mr. Wilson looked off into the distance like he wasn't seeing the cornfields, but what used to be there. "Mrs. Franklin, now there's another one who never sold—even after the house burned down. She said wasn't no way she was going to let them turn her paradise into a big corn patch."

"Might get turned into something worse than a corn patch," Luther said, "if that developer does what he says he's going to do."

"Yes," Mr. Wilson said in a heavy voice. "That would be a heap worse."

When they got the plants to the Wilson house and put them out on the back porch, Chip figured he and Luther still had a chance to spend half an hour or so in the Jungle before dark. But Mrs. Wilson insisted on giving them a glass of iced tea, and then Ruby came in and told Luther that it was too late for him to be running off. She always made sure he got a head start on his homework every weekend.

Ruby was a lot stricter about grades than Chip's mom, who didn't make a fuss as long as Chip didn't make anything under a C. Fortunately Luther was a fast reader and good at math, so he generally got the kind of grades Ruby expected. Chip got mostly Cs, or sometimes, accidentally, a B. The only subject where he regularly got an A was science, and that was because it was his favorite subject, especially the way Mr. O'Dell taught it.

When Chip finally started for home, the sun was already on the horizon. He ached to turn down the dirt track to the Old Place and look for the kittens, but he decided against it. He didn't want to be in the Jungle when it got dark. He turned into his driveway just as Kate was heading out to the goat shed to do the milking. He cut across the yard and took one of the milk buckets from his sister.

"I'll milk Go-Girl," Chip said, even though it wasn't his turn. On the walk home he'd been thinking about something he wanted to discuss with Kate. He figured she'd be more agreeable if he did a few favors for her first.

"Thanks!" Kate said.

Chip put out grain for all three goats, then he and Kate each took a stool and started squirting milk into their buckets. Chip had once tried milking a cow and didn't much like it. A cow's four teats are small and it's hard to grip them in the right way to make the milk come out. Goats only have two big teats, very easy to handle. Also, goats don't give as much milk as cows, so it only takes a couple of minutes to milk one. When they were finished, Chip and Kate carried the buckets of milk into the kitchen. By the time they'd finished straining the milk to take out any mosquitoes or bits of hay or goat hair that might have fallen in, Mom was home from work.

Chip set the table without being asked, then put the goat milk and butter and cornbread on the table. Kate took a big pot of vegetable-beef stew off the stove and filled their bowls. As soon as they all sat down, Kate started talking to Mom about the only subject she ever talked about anymore—Ruby's wedding.

"Ruby has decided to have a garden wedding," Kate announced.

Chip opened his mouth to make a crack about how if Ruby went dragging a wedding gown through their vegetable garden, Mrs. Wilson would probably whack off the tail of the dress with a hoe. Then he remembered that this wasn't a good time to annoy his sister, so he kept his mouth shut.

Mom smiled dreamily. "Mrs. Wilson's flowers are so pretty in June. Are they inviting many people?"

"Not many," Kate told her. "Just a few of Richard's friends from school and some of the Wilsons' friends from church. Plus the Hashimotos...and us, of course."

When supper was over, Chip washed the dishes and Kate dried them. She and Mom kept on yapping about the wedding. Chip smiled to himself, enjoying all the wisecracks about weddings that came into his head.

Once the kitchen was cleaned up, Kate went to her room and Mom went to take her bath. Chip stuck his head into his sister's room and asked, "Kate? Can I talk to you?"

"*May* I talk to you. Yes, Chip, you *may*."

Chip perched on the edge of her bed and watched as Kate rummaged through a dresser drawer. "Do you have a date with Brad tonight?" he asked.

"Tomorrow morning," Kate said. "We're going to the lake. So what is it you want to talk to me about?"

"The Old Place," Chip said. "That builder guy is going to wreck it."

"That's *awful!*" She pulled a blue T-shirt from the drawer. Chip couldn't tell whether she meant the Old Place getting wrecked was awful or the shirt was awful.

"Our rabbits are there," he said sadly. "And the barn owls, and a zillion other birds' nests. If their homes get destroyed, the babies will die."

Kate threw the shirt back in the drawer and started brushing her hair. Chip saw that she was watching him instead of looking at herself in the mirror. She put her hairbrush on the dresser and came to sit beside him on the bed.

"Chip, I know you feel terrible about the Old Place," she said. "So do I. But there's nothing we can do about it."

He took a deep breath. "Yes, there is," he said.

Kate smiled. "Like what?"

"We're going to protest."

Kate's eyes lit up with interest. "Who's 'we'?"

"A bunch of us kids. Mr. O'Dell took my class out there on a field trip, and everyone loved it."

"Hmm," Kate said. "When's this protest going to take place?"

"Tuesday," Chip said. "That's when Mr. Blake plans to bring the bulldozer."

"This is *really* interesting."

Chip had thought his sister might help him out somehow, but he hadn't expected her to be so enthusiastic. What she said next told him why.

"Ever since Brad became a reporter on the school paper, he's been trying to get the town paper to let him do feature articles. He wants to get some real newspaper experience before he graduates. But they keep blowing him off, saying nobody's interested in school stuff, except for sports. Maybe"—Kate gave Chip a big smile—"they'd be interested in this."

"I was kind of hoping Brad would be interested," Chip said.

Actually, Brad's writing an article about the protest hadn't crossed his mind. Chip had hoped to get Brad involved for a totally different reason. Brad had a *car*. And not a little one either. Because of the way his divorced parents were always trying to outdo each other, when Brad's mom had offered to buy him a Honda Civic, his dad had rushed out and bought him an SUV.

"The only problem," Chip explained to Kate, "is that we need a way to get the kids from school out to the Old Place."

When Chip said that, it was like a lightbulb flashed on in Kate's head. "Oh my gosh, Chip! Are you talking about *ditching school?*"

"Well, yeah," Chip started. "How else—?"

"And you want Brad to drive a bunch of *elementary* kids to an illegal protest?"

"Who said it was illegal?" Chip didn't like the way Kate had said *elementary* kids, like they were in diapers or something.

"It's illegal if you ditch school!" Kate said flatly. "You know Brad got expelled once, and he'd *never* do anything that might get him expelled again."

"Then I guess he won't get the story." Chip spoke defiantly, like the protest would happen anyway. But the truth was that getting Brad to transport them was the only way his plan would work. He'd been depending on Kate to convince Brad. Realizing that he couldn't depend on her or on anybody else caused Chip's throat to tighten up.

Kate must have seen the disappointed look before he ducked his head, because she put her arm around his shoulder and said, "I'm sorry, Chip. But there really isn't any way to stop that developer, not if he's got a permit to build there."

"We *have* to stop him," Chip said, "because more than rabbits live out there."

"What do you mean?" Kate's voice suddenly got suspicious. "Has some homeless person moved into that old barn?"

"Of course not," Chip said. "The roof's all caved in."

"Who, then?"

Chip looked at his sister, needing to trust her but afraid he couldn't. "Something special," he said. "Maybe the most special thing in the state of Florida."

"O-kaay." Kate sounded like she was holding back a laugh. "Why don't you tell me all about this most special thing." She scooted back on the bed and crossed her long legs in front of her.

Chip turned to face her. "I can't tell you," he said, although he'd already decided that he would have to. "Because this is something that even Brad can't know about. And I *know* you'd tell him."

Kate frowned. "Not necessarily. Girls don't tell their boyfriends *every*thing."

"But you would want to tell him this," Chip insisted, "because it would be newsworthy. Even more than our protest."

"Newsworthy?" Kate asked. "Who else knows about it?"

"Luther and me. And Lily, but she's only heard about it. She hasn't seen it yet."

"So are you going to tell me?"

"No," said Chip. "Because I can't trust you."

"Chip!" Kate exclaimed, looking truly hurt. "What a *terrible* thing to say. When have I ever told something I promised not to?"

"That's right," Chip said thoughtfully. "You never told anybody about us goatnapping Little Billy."

Kate's cheeks reddened. "No," she said, lowering her voice. "And you better not ever tell either. We could still get into a *lot* of trouble if anybody found out." Kate was quiet for a minute, then she said, "All right, I promise. I will not tell Brad."

"And you won't tell Ruby? Or Mom? Or anybody?"

"Nobody," Kate promised. "Not a single soul."

So Chip told her about the wild kittens on the Old Place. As he described them, Kate's eyes got bigger and bigger. "We think they're Florida panthers," he told her. "Lily saw some kittens just like these on TV, and Luther looked them up on the Internet. There are only maybe fifty wild Florida panthers left in the whole world, and most of them are in the Everglades."

Kate grabbed the sides of her head like she was trying to keep it from exploding. "Oh, Chip!" she said in a scared whisper. "Don't you realize how dangerous it is for you to go there? If those kittens really are panthers, there must be a panther mother close by. A full-grown panther can *kill* a person."

"I don't think these kittens have a mother. At least I've never seen her, or any big tracks. I think they're orphans."

Kate was quiet for a minute. Chip didn't want to give her any more time to think about it. "So will you help us, Kate?" he pleaded. "Will you ask Brad if he'll give us a ride from school to the Old Place on Tuesday morning so we can stop the bulldozer?"

Kate twisted a strand of hair around and around her forefinger, the way she did when she was trying to figure something out. "Okay," she said finally. "On one condition."

"What?"

"You show me the kittens."

Chip wasn't quick to agree. He knew that every extra person who went tramping in to see the kittens made it less likely that *he'd* get to see them. But what choice did he have?

"Okay," Chip said at last. "Tomorrow morning."

"Not in the morning. I told you, Brad and I are going to the lake. Maybe later, in the afternoon?"

"Okay. And you'll tell Brad about the protest and ask if he'll drive us there?"

"I'll tell him about the protest, but I won't ask him to ditch class to drive you kids there—not until you prove to me that there are actual Florida panther kittens living on the Old Place."

"Thanks, Kate!" Chip leapt off the bed and headed for the door. Then he turned and said, "You're my favorite sister."

"Yeah, right," she said with a big grin. "I'm also your *only* sister."

16

Chicken Necks

Lily showed up a few minutes after Chip's mother left for the nursery. She was wearing jeans instead of soccer shorts, and she had a small backpack dangling from one shoulder. Chip was about to go milk the goats, so he handed her a bucket. When they got to the goat pen, he tried to get Lily to milk Brown Sugar, who gave the least milk, but Lily insisted on milking Honey, her favorite. Chip finished milking the other two and was standing around waiting for Lily to finish when Luther walked up.

"What's taking you so long?" Luther asked.

"Chores," Chip said, and jerked his head at Lily, who was still milking.

"I'm just about finished," Lily called.

"What're the books for?" Chip asked, indicating the two Luther was carrying.

"Reading," Luther said. He held up a library book called *The Florida Panther*. "It's for little kids," Luther said. "But it has good pictures."

Lily came out of the pen with her bucket of milk. "What's the other one?"

Luther turned the paperback right side up so they could see the cover.

"*Pelé: My Life and the Beautiful Game,*" Chip read aloud.

"Not Pelé the soccer player?" Lily asked, snatching the book out of Luther's hand.

Luther grinned. "Booker gave it to me. I brought it along for you to read, Lily, while we're waiting for the kittens to come out. I couldn't see you staying quiet for two or three hours."

"Stop reading and look where you're going," Chip warned Lily. "If you spill that milk, Kate'll have a fit."

Lily laughed and went in the back door ahead of the boys. She set down the bucket of milk, put the book in her pack, then took out a small plastic bag. "Guess what I brought?" Before they had a chance to guess, she announced, "A chicken neck."

"What for?" Chip and Luther stared at her, waiting for the punch line.

"My mom saves chicken necks in the freezer, to make soup," Lily explained. "I brought this for the kittens. If they smell chicken, maybe they'll come out sooner and I won't have to sit still for two hours."

Kate wandered into the kitchen. "Morning, munchkins," she said. She still acted as if Chip and his friends were six-year-olds, even though he and Luther were almost as tall as she was. "Where are you off to this morning?"

"Just...around," Chip said. He shoved the others out the back door before Kate could mention their conversation from last night. He wanted to be the one who told them about his idea.

Once they'd turned down Lost Goat Lane, Chip ran the whole plan past Luther and Lily.

Luther looked dumbstruck. "You told her we had a *bunch* of protesters? We haven't asked *anybody* yet!"

"I didn't say how many. You and Lily ought to be able to recruit a few people. We *might* end up with a bunch."

"We might," Lily agreed. "But what we really need is an adult to be our spokesperson. Nobody pays any attention to kids."

"Half-adults was the best I could do," Chip muttered.

Luther laughed. "I like that. Kate and Brad—half-adults."

"We don't have Brad yet," Chip reminded him. "And we might not get him if Kate doesn't see the kittens this afternoon."

"Well, *I'm* going to see them," Lily said, reaching around to pat her backpack. "That's what the chicken neck is for."

Chip thought she sounded pretty confident, given that she'd never owned a cat, hadn't seen these particular kittens, and didn't know whether they liked raw chicken or not. But he didn't say anything.

They jumped the ditch and walked through the woods till they came out on the grassy knoll. Butterflies zigzagged through the air, and dragonflies with see-through wings were hovering over the pond. It was the most beautiful place Chip had ever seen, and judging by the quietness of the other two, they must have felt the same way.

Lily slipped off her pack and took out the chicken neck. "Where should I put it?"

Chip thought for a moment, then nodded toward the woods. "Twice before, I saw them come out on that side. Put it a little distance from the trees, so they'll have to come out to get it." He turned around. "And we'll sit here," he said, pointing to an old log lying on the ground, close enough to the edge of the forest that they'd be in the shade.

After Lily laid the chicken neck in the grass, they all sat in a row with their backs against the old log. Lily only watched for about five minutes, then started reading the book about the famous Brazilian soccer player. Luther quietly leafed through the kids' book about Florida panthers. Chip read the pages as Luther turned them, and they both studied the pictures. After they'd finished, Luther and Chip just sat there observing, the way Mr. O'Dell had taught his students to do when they were in the field.

As it happened, Chip was looking the opposite way when the kittens did appear, so Luther saw them first. Luther squeezed Chip's wrist and Chip turned his head slowly so he could see where Luther was looking. In front of them, a kitten was sniffing at the chicken neck. Chip nudged Lily's shoulder. She took in a quick breath and stared.

The second kitten, a little smaller than the first, was slinking out of the woods. It grabbed the chicken neck in its teeth, dragged it a few feet, then shook its head comically from side to side. The bigger kitten tried to take the chicken neck, but the little one held on, growling loudly. It was all Chip could do to keep from laughing out loud. The kittens, who looked like fuzzy stuffed toys, were growling as if they were the biggest, meanest tigers in the jungle. The little kitten tried to run with the chicken neck, but it dragged on the ground, slowing the kitten down. The big one caught up and pounced from behind. The chicken neck dropped to the ground, and the kittens rolled over and over, tussling, until one remembered the chicken neck and dashed back to grab it. Eventually they reached the woods with it and disappeared from sight.

Although the children waited in silence for nearly an hour, the panther kittens never reappeared. Finally Chip looked up. The sun was high in the sky. "Nearly noon. Gotta go get Kate."

They bushwhacked out to the cornfield and sprinted down

the rows until they reached the road. "Do you think the kittens saw us?" Luther asked, stopping to get his breath.

"I don't know," Chip said.

"If we brought a chicken neck every day and put it a little closer to us each time, they'd get used to us," Lily suggested. "They'd see that we weren't going to bother them."

"That's more or less what we did with the rabbits," Chip reminded them.

"But the only one that ever let us pet her was Miz Rabbit," Lily pointed out. "I want to *pet* those kittens."

"No!" Chip said firmly. "They're wild animals. Mr. O'Dell says scientists shouldn't interfere with the wildlife they're observing."

"Right," Luther seconded. "Go pet your soccer ball."

But from the look on her face, Chip could tell that for once in her life Lily wasn't thinking about soccer. She set her jaw. If the boys were going back to the Jungle with Kate, Chip knew that Lily was going back too.

17
Half-Adult Help

When they reached Chip's house, Kate was waiting. "Hey!" she exclaimed when she saw Lily. "You look cute in jeans."

"I don't dress to be 'cute,'" Lily said, eyeing Kate's shorts and tank top. "And you'd better not either, unless you want to get all scratched up."

"Oh! Right." Kate went to her room and came back a few minutes later in jeans and a tank top, with a long-sleeved shirt tied around her waist.

By then Chip, Luther, and Lily had chugged down glasses of lemonade and made peanut butter sandwiches. They wolfed them down and headed straight back to the Jungle, this time with Kate.

They jumped the ditch and pushed through the ragweed. They'd only taken a few steps into the forest when Kate let out a yelp. "There it is! I saw it!"

"What?" the others all asked at once. "Where?"

"The panther kitten!" she exclaimed. "Over there! It ran under that bush!"

Chip looked where she was pointing, then laughed so hard he had to hold his stomach. "Kate," he gasped, "that wasn't a panther. That was an armadillo. See here?" Chip pointed to a muddy place the animal had crossed. "There are its tracks."

"Oh. I just saw that it was tan like a panther and thought—"

"The kittens aren't tan," Luther explained. "They're spotted. Also," he added with a grin, "they have fur and fuzzy tails, not shells and skinny rat tails."

"Come on," Chip said. "And *be quiet*. No more talking, okay?"

Everyone got quiet then, and they moved as silently as possible through the forest until they emerged into the clearing. Kate, like everyone else upon seeing the grassy knoll and swampy little pond for the first time, caught her breath in wonder.

She nudged Luther. "What's that?" She mouthed the question without making a sound.

The big black bird sat atop its usual dead tree stump perch with its wings outspread to catch the sun.

"Anhinga," Luther mouthed back.

Chip held his finger to his lips and pointed to the old log. "Sit," he whispered. Luther and Lily sat down and leaned back against the log. Chip dropped down between them. Kate moved a short distance away and sat on the grass with her legs crossed in front of her.

Half an hour passed and absolutely nothing happened except that the anhinga flew away and the two snowy white egrets sailed in. They stalked slowly through the shallow water, occasionally stabbing something with their long beaks. Chip started to worry that Kate would get impatient and leave. He wished that Lily had brought along an extra chicken neck. He squeezed his eyes shut. *Please, kittens,* he repeated in his mind. *Please. Won't at least one of you come out?*

When he opened his eyes, he thought he must have fallen asleep and was dreaming. One kitten was waddling in its klutzy way through the tall meadow grass, right toward Kate! Kate was looking directly at it, not moving a muscle. The kitten got to within about two feet of her, and then she did the absolute wrong thing—she reached out to touch it.

The kitten leapt straight up in the air and somersaulted backwards, hissing like a snake and showing a whole mouthful of sharp little teeth. The suddenness of its movement—and the hiss—caused all of them to jump. They laughed aloud as the kitten went racing through the grass and into the forest.

"Did you see that?" Lily exclaimed. "Boy, could I use a move like that in soccer!"

"You shouldn't have tried to touch it!" Chip scolded Kate. "You scared it!"

Kate was still staring at the spot where the kitten had been, like she couldn't believe it had actually been there. "I just wanted to pet it," she whispered.

"You don't pet wild animals," Luther repeated what Mr. O'Dell always told his class. "You shouldn't interfere with them at all."

"That's right," Chip said. Secretly he was glad Kate had frightened the kitten away. After all, he was the one who had discovered them, and if anybody got to touch one, it ought to be *him*. After all the time he'd spent sitting still and observing, it would have been totally unfair if Kate, who hadn't been waiting even one hour, had touched a kitten first.

"Will they come back?" Kate asked.

Chip shrugged. "They never have before. Usually we get one glimpse of them, then they disappear. This morning we waited almost an hour after we first saw them, but they didn't come back." Chip stood up. "I think we should go."

"Already?" Luther looked at him in surprise, but Chip just gave him a look that said, *Come on, I'll explain later.*

To Kate he said, "Now that you know there really are panther kittens here, will you talk to Brad?"

Kate glanced at her watch. "You can talk to him yourself. He'll be here in half an hour."

"Here?" Chip, Luther, and Lily yelled in unison.

"Kate!" Chip was furious. "You promised!"

"Not *here*," Kate defended herself. "I didn't tell him anything about this place. He's meeting us out front, by the old barn. So you can show him where you plan to do your protest."

"Oh." Chip breathed a sigh of relief. "That's okay."

Together they trekked out of the Jungle and through the cornfield to the front of the Old Place. Chip hadn't thought to bring any grain, but Lily, as usual, had a pocketful of corn chips, which she scattered in the grass. Then they sat in the shade of the barn and waited for the rabbits. By the time Brad's SUV drove up, there were fourteen of them nibbling at the chips.

To Chip, Brad looked pretty much the same as he always had, a tall boy with straight brown hair, short on the sides but longish on top. A lock of his hair flopped over his forehead, so he was constantly tossing it back to keep it out of his eyes. Chip had always thought of Brad as sort of geeky, but he had to admit that something about him had changed. He looked a lot surer of himself, and he had big arm muscles, which you would expect of somebody who was the high school baseball team's top pitcher.

Kate went to meet him, and Brad put an arm around her shoulder. Together they walked toward the barn, then stopped a few yards from it. Brad took a camera out of his shirt pocket and began snapping pictures.

When Brad had enough photos of the rabbits, Chip asked him if he wanted to see the barn owl's nest.

Of course he did, so they went into the old barn and put the ladder into position so they could climb to the loft. When everyone was up, they pulled the ladder into the loft and leaned it against a roof beam so they could climb to where the owl's nest was. The owl mother had gone off somewhere, so it was no problem for Brad to take all the pictures he wanted.

Baby barn owls are not like other birds. They're big, and they don't seem frightened when you pick them up. The year before, when there were other owl babies, Chip, Luther, and Lily had climbed the ladder often and taken them out of the nest just to feel their soft, furlike feathers. After Mr. O'Dell had told his class that wild animals were afraid of humans—whether they showed it or not—the kids had pretty much left the owls alone. Brad stood on the ladder and took lots more pictures.

Then they trooped out of the barn and over to the foundations of the old house. Chip showed Brad the mockingbird's nest in an old orange tree, but warned him not to try to take pictures of it. "If you get anywhere near the tree," he said, "the mother mockingbird will dive-bomb you."

Brad grinned. "I know. A pair of mockingbirds nest in the orange tree in our backyard every year. My mom hates them, because from the time the babies hatch till they fly away, the mother mockingbird attacks her every time she goes out the back door."

"Come over here." Lily motioned Brad toward a hibiscus bush. "The red-winged blackbirds don't make a fuss if you look in their nest, as long as you don't touch anything." Brad took a few pictures of her looking into the nest, which last week held blue-speckled eggs, but now had two baby birds.

"So what part of the place is the guy planning to build on?" Brad asked.

"All of it, back to the trees," Chip explained. "He said he'd leave the woods till later. He's going to grade this front part, where the house and barn and pasture used to be, down to bare dirt and build a meatpacking plant."

Brad took a notebook out of his pocket and jotted down notes while Chip and Luther talked. He wrote down Mr. Blake's name and what he'd said about the old lady living in a nursing home. He was especially interested when they told him that Mr. Blake had said Mrs. Franklin had leased the place to him only because he promised to clean it up.

Brad grinned. "If I can get him to tell me that, I'll quote him in my article."

"He probably won't be as open with you as he was with Mr. O'Dell," Kate pointed out. "Not if he knows you're with the press."

Brad shrugged. "We'll see. I think I've got the makings of a good story here anyway."

"So will you help us?" Chip asked.

Brad turned in a slow circle, taking in all of the Old Place and the fields around it. "I think I know a good angle for the article. This is the only place for miles where wild animals can live. Cornfields and cane fields are always getting plowed under or burned, which kills any wildlife that happens to be there. About the only safe place left for wild animals in South Florida is the Everglades, and it's a lot smaller than it used to be."

Chip, Luther, and Lily looked at each other. Brad really hadn't answered the question. Just then, Miz Rabbit hopped up to Luther and began sniffing around his sneakers. He knelt and scratched between her ears.

Brad looked down at Luther and Miz Rabbit. "These animals really trust you, don't they? They haven't learned that there are some people you can't trust."

"Yes, they have," Chip said. "But they trust us anyway. Because we've never hurt them."

"And we're not going to let anybody else hurt them either," Lily said defiantly.

"We're going to protect them," Luther said.

"But we need help," Chip said, looking up at Brad.

Brad snapped one last picture of Luther petting Miz Rabbit, then dropped his camera into his shirt pocket. "Okay," he said. "I'll help."

Kate put her arm around Brad's waist. "So, where do you want Brad to pick up you troublemakers on Tuesday?"

Before Brad and Kate left, Lily asked them for a ride to the community center. She figured there was still time for a soccer game, or at least a few practice drills. She tried to get Chip and Luther to come with her, but they shook their heads.

"Too late in the afternoon," Chip said, and Luther nodded his agreement.

But the minute the others had gone, Luther looked at Chip and said, "Back to the Jungle?"

Chip smiled. "If it's just us and we're super quiet, the kittens might come out again."

"Yeah. I'd like to take a few pictures of my own." Luther reached into his backpack, took out a camera, and handed it to Chip. "What do you think of this?"

Chip examined the camera. "Nice! Is it new?"

Luther shook his head. "Mama's old one. Mr. Jackson gave her a new digital for her birthday, and she gave me this one. I ruined a few rolls of films learning how to set the shutter speed and stuff like that, but I've been reading the book that came with it. Old technology. But I'm getting the hang of it."

It was around four thirty in the afternoon when Chip and Luther got back to the Jungle. They settled down with their backs against the log and waited. The anhinga and the snowy white egrets didn't show up. For the longest time it seemed like nothing was moving around the pond except the butter-flies and dragonflies.

At last there was a rustling in the edge of the forest and a flash of tan, but what came out wasn't a panther kitten. It was the armadillo. When it waddled down to the edge of the water to drink, Luther zoomed in on it and snapped several pictures. The armadillo snuffled around for a bit, then disappeared back into the woods.

A fairly large turtle parked itself on a cypress knee sticking out of the water. But before Luther could focus his camera on it, it dove into the water and disappeared.

Chip was beginning to get restless. It was that time of day, just before sunset, when mosquitoes seem most hungry. After Luther slapped one away, he quietly reached into his backpack and came out with a bottle of insect repellent. Chip knew what that meant. Luther was not going to leave until he saw the kit-tens or it was too dark to take pictures. Chip smeared his bare skin with repellent and handed the bottle back to Luther, who rubbed some on his arms and face. Then they settled back against the log to wait some more.

The waiting gave Chip time to think. The more he thought about what was going to happen in the very near future, the more depressed he got. It saddened him to realize that if he and Luther had been just a little more adventurous, they would have discovered this pond four years ago, when they first picked the Old Place as their hideout.

Chip could tell it was nearing sunset because the clearing had been in shadow for a while. Overhead, a few clouds were changing from white to pink. He was admiring the way the rose-colored clouds were reflected in the water when he heard

Luther suck wind. Chip quickly scanned the area but didn't see any movement. Then he spotted one of the kittens on its belly, creeping through the grass. It was sneaking up on the other kitten—which Chip didn't see until the first one landed on the second one's back—and the two of them shot into the air like balls of fuzz. Then they tumbled back into the grass and went rolling end over end. By the time the two kittens had wrestled each other into the trees, Luther's camera had clicked a dozen times—one picture right after the other, each one with a flash. Then the kittens were gone.

Luther turned to Chip and gave him a high five. They stood up, laughing with excitement.

"Wow!" Chip exclaimed. "They're so fast! Think you got some good shots?"

"Maybe. I had it set at a fast shutter speed."

"We ought to do like Lily said, always bring snacks and put them closer and closer till the kittens come right up to us!"

"Then I'd get some even better pictures!" Luther said excitedly. "Think about it, Chip! We might be the only kids in the *world* who ever got pictures of panther kittens in the wild!"

As they made their way back through the dark woods, Luther kept up a constant chatter. He couldn't wait to get the film developed. Chip, on the other hand, hardly said a word. He was glad about the pictures, but he wanted *more* than pictures. He wanted the actual kittens to stay right there so someday he and they might get to be friends. But the only way that could happen was by stopping the developers from destroying this last, secret wild place.

18
Blue Monday

When Chip got off the bus Monday morning, he went straight to his classroom instead of dawdling outside until the last minute. Mr. O'Dell was sitting at his desk grading papers.

"Mr. O'Dell?" Chip said.

"Oh, hi, Chip," the teacher said, flipping through the stack of papers. He pulled one out and held it up. It was the observation notes Chip had turned in after their field trip. He'd written about the ants that had attacked Mr. O'Dell that day at the Old Place.

"I wish I'd known how aggressive these particular ants were before I went messing around in their territory," Mr. O'Dell said with a grin. Then he moved his thumb off the top corner of the paper to show a big fat A.

The A, along with Mr. O'Dell's friendly smile, gave Chip confidence, so he said right out, "Mr. O'Dell, sir, I need to ask you a favor."

"What kind of favor?"

"You know those developers we saw out at the Old Place?" Chip said. "They're coming tomorrow morning to grade it down to bare earth."

"Barbarians!" Mr. O'Dell said angrily. "They sure didn't

waste any time, did they? Too bad we can't stop them."

Chip almost got angry himself, he was so sick of hearing people say the developers couldn't be stopped. "But we *can* stop them!" he said, a little more loudly than he had intended. "We can *protest.*"

"Oh?" Mr. O'Dell arched his eyebrows. "Who's we?"

"I was thinking…that is…I was hoping maybe you'd come with us? Us kids, I mean. We need a grown-up because, you know, just kids…" His voice trailed off.

Mr. O'Dell paused a moment, looking down at the stack of papers. "I'd like to help, Chip. I really would," he said softly. "But teachers can't afford to get involved in controversial issues. I could lose my job for something like that."

"Oh." They were both quiet, Mr. O'Dell staring at the papers on his desk and Chip staring at his feet. Then Chip remembered what else he was supposed to ask Mr. O'Dell.

"What about the kids?" he asked.

Mr. O'Dell frowned. "What do you mean?"

"Can we ask the class if any of them want to come with us to protest?"

Mr. O'Dell swallowed a couple of times and didn't answer. Chip figured no answer probably meant *no.* He felt let down. Also a little bit stubborn. He decided he'd just stand right there in front of Mr. O'Dell's desk all day if he had to, until Mr. O'Dell said yes or no.

But Mr. O'Dell didn't say either one. Suddenly he stood up. "I have to take some papers to the office," he said. "The bell's probably going to ring before I get back. What you say to the class while I'm gone, well—" He gave Chip a weak grin. "I guess I can't stop you if I'm not here." Heading for the door, Mr. O'Dell added, "And it's probably a good idea if nobody tells me what went on when I was out of the room."

"Yes sir!"

The bell rang as Mr. O'Dell went out the door, and kids started pouring in. Chip grabbed Lily and pulled her to the side. "He's going to be out of the room for a few minutes," he whispered. "You have to ask while he's gone, because he doesn't want to know anything about it."

Lily looked disgusted. "So he's not going to help us?"

"Too controversial. He'll lose his job."

"Wimp," she muttered.

"Go ahead, quick! Ask before he gets back."

"I will as soon as they get in their seats!" Lily snapped. "Half of them aren't here yet." She went to the front of the room, ready to speak up as soon as the students settled down. When most of the kids were in their seats, Lily put two fingers in her mouth and let out one of her earsplitting whistles. In the moment of quiet that followed, she said, "We need volunteers to help us fight some murderers."

The kids looked at her like she had lost her marbles. Some of them laughed. But Lily kept talking. "You know that old farm where we went on our field trip? Tomorrow some guys are going to come with bulldozers. They're going to mow down all the bushes that have birds' nests in them, and they're going to knock down the old barn and kill the barn owls. They're even going to bulldoze the meadow where the rabbit burrows are and all the baby bunnies will get buried alive." Lily barely paused for breath. "We're organizing a protest. We're planning to go out there in the morning and stop them. Who wants to come?"

Only two hands went up: Chip's and Luther's.

Lily waited a few seconds. "Anyone else?"

Tamara asked, "Is this a school-sanctioned field trip?"

"No," Lily said. "It's a kid-sanctioned trip."

"You're talking about ditching school?" somebody asked.

"Yeah, but for a really good reason," Lily insisted. "If we don't stop the bulldozer, most of those animals will get killed."

"If I ditch school, *I'll* get killed," said another kid.

"Me too," other voices said.

Lily waited another minute, then asked again, "Anybody?"

There was dead silence for about half a second, then a boy in the back row said that rabbits were pests anyway and made a joke about going out there and collecting bulldozer-flattened rabbits for people to hang on the rearview mirrors of their cars. Some kids around him laughed, and everybody started talking at once. Lily threw up her hands and stalked back to her seat, muttering, "What a bunch of jerks."

Chip was feeling let down himself, so he knew how Lily must feel. She might even feel worse than he did. At least his letdown was private, not in front of the whole class. But either way it came to the same thing: They were on their own.

Then Chip remembered one last chance for help. When they'd gotten off the bus, Luther had gone straight over to a group of community center kids and started talking to them. But several of those kids were in this class, and not one of them had responded to Lily's request for volunteers. Had everyone turned Luther down too?

Chip looked over at Luther and raised his eyebrows. Luther gave a slight shrug. Chip didn't know what that meant and couldn't ask because just then Mr. O'Dell came back into the room and reminded the class that it was time to stop socializing and get to work.

Chip didn't have a chance to ask Luther about the community center kids until they were in the lunch line. Luther told him that they hadn't made up their minds.

They got their trays and headed for a table. They spotted

some of the kids from the center sitting together at a table by the windows. Chip followed Luther and took a seat across from Kishan and Jesse, the two he knew best.

Ruben was there too, even though he was a fifth grader and was supposed to be at an entirely different table. When Chip first met Ruben, he thought he'd probably been held back a couple of times, because he was as big as a seventh grader. But as far as Chip could tell, it wasn't stupidity that had kept Ruben from doing well in school; it was his attitude. His tough-guy attitude showed all the time, even when he was laughing, like now.

"I might go," Ruben told Luther. "I always wanted to take on a bulldozer."

"Uh, we want to keep it nonviolent," Luther said.

"Oh." Ruben looked disappointed. "Not even rocks?"

"Takes more courage to put your body on the line," Lily told him. "Like, remember those Chinese students in Tiananmen Square? There was this one guy who stood right in front of an army tank and it couldn't go forward without squashing him."

"Did it?" several of the kids asked at once.

"I don't know," Lily admitted. "I think someone pulled him away before he got run over. Anyway, the picture of him standing in front of the tank is very famous."

"I'd rather be a live person than a famous picture," Kishan mumbled.

The talk went on like that until the bell rang. Chip returned to his class still not knowing whether even one of the community center kids would participate. As the day wore on, he got more and more depressed. What kind of protest would it be with just him and Lily and Luther?

After school they walked to the community center and

headed straight for the soccer field. When the game ended, everyone flopped in the grass on the shady side of the building. Chip and Lily looked at Luther, wondering when he was going to bring up the subject of the protest.

Luther finally stood up and faced the group. "So," he said, "any of you going out to the Old Place with us tomorrow morning to see if we can stop the bulldozers?"

"I'll go," Ruben said. "If a Chinese kid can stop a tank with his bare hands, I can stand up to a little old bulldozer." He laughed. "As long as the driver doesn't have a gun."

Ralph laughed too, and said, "You can count me in." That was no surprise, because Ralph always went along with whatever Ruben decided.

No one spoke for a moment, then Kishan, who'd been on the field trip, said, "I'll go. I really liked those rabbits and I don't think it's fair to destroy their homes."

"What about you?" Luther asked Miguel.

Miguel shook his head. "Not my problem, man. My mom and me, we're only here on a temporary visa. We have nowhere to go now, and if we get kicked out of the U.S., we'd *really* have nowhere to go."

"It's the same with the animals," Jesse said. "They're gonna get blasted by the bulldozer just like we got blasted by the hurricane, and they got no place to go either."

"Okay," Luther said finally, when it was obvious that nobody else was going to volunteer. "Brad, a kid from the high school, is going to drive us out there in his SUV. He'll pick up Chip and Lily and me at school as soon as the bus gets in. You all wait on the corner of Second and Elm and we'll pick you up there. Better than coming to school and maybe getting caught trying to leave."

"What if you don't show up?" Ruben asked.

"It'll mean we got caught. But that's not going to happen," Chip said, sounding a lot more confident than he felt. He could already imagine a teacher waving down Brad's SUV before it got out of the parking lot and hauling them all off to the principal's office.

"If we're not there by eight o'clock," Luther said, "you go on to school. Nobody will know you were involved, so you'll just get dinged for being late."

"They're gonna know we're involved in something if we're gone all morning," Ralph reminded them. "We'll all get slapped with detention for that."

"Right," Luther agreed. "And if our parents find out, they're going to go ballistic."

"But our parents might never know," Chip pointed out. "Teachers don't normally contact parents about a tardy. Not the first time, anyway."

"What'll we tell the teachers when they ask why we're late?" Ralph asked.

"Slept in?" Ruben offered.

"Got chased up a tree by a vicious dog?" suggested Kishan.

"Tell them it's personal problems," Luther said. "You don't have to go into any details."

"So how many of you are with us?" Lily asked.

"Yo," answered Ruben.

"Me too," Ralph and Kishan said at the same time.

Jesse and a girl named Letoria brought the total to five.

Chip, Luther, and Lily exchanged looks. It wasn't as many as they had hoped, but Luther's friends had come through for them where their own classmates hadn't. Chip felt a sudden rush of gratitude. Because of the community center kids, this blue Monday now seemed much brighter.

19
The Protest

Chip had just taken his seat on the bus Tuesday morning when a flatbed truck hauling a bulldozer rolled down the highway from the opposite direction. Looking back, he saw it turn down Lost Goat Lane. From that moment, Chip could hardly sit still. He had never realized how *slow* a school bus traveled. At the rate they were going, the Old Place could be flattened before they even got there!

The minute the bus pulled to a stop in front of the school, Chip saw Brad's SUV at the end of the parking lot, partially hidden between a building and a row of tall shrubs. He whispered to Luther and Lily to get a move on, and together they crowded into the aisle and pushed their way forward.

"Slow down," Kate warned in a low voice as she got off the bus behind them. "Go along the wall of the building and around to the back of the SUV. Brad said he'd leave the back door open. Get in and lie down."

Trying to look casual, they walked to the SUV and slipped into the back. Kate got in the passenger side and slid down in the seat so she couldn't be seen.

"Where are the others?" Brad asked.

"Waiting at the corner of Second and Elm," Chip answered. "Hurry, Brad! The bulldozer is already there!"

"No!" Kate said. "Don't go fast! It'll attract attention."

"No sweat," Brad said. "Once we get out of the parking lot, we're home free."

Two minutes later, Brad pulled to a stop at the corner of Second and Elm. Doors opened, and Ruben, Ralph, Letoria, and Jesse crowded into the backseat. Kishan and Miguel squirmed into the back next to Chip, Luther, and Lily.

"Hey, Miguel!" Lily exclaimed. "What're you doing here? I thought you said this wasn't your problem."

"It's not my problem," Miguel said with a shy smile. "But it is my team."

"Is this it?" Brad called back. "This is what you call *a whole bunch?*"

"It's the best bunch we could find," Chip informed him.

Ruben laughed in his boisterous way. "And we're a tough bunch. We're gonna stop that bulldozer in its tracks!"

Chip put his head down on the carpeted floor, closed his eyes, and hoped they wouldn't be too late.

Brad stopped a little distance away from the Old Place and told everybody to get out. "You have to walk from here," he said. "It wouldn't be professional for a reporter to take people to a protest. I'll come later, once there's some action to cover."

"Drive me around to the other side," Kate instructed. "I'm going to slip in the other way, so they don't see me."

"I didn't know you were going to protest with us!" Chip exclaimed.

"How are you going to protest without being seen?" Lily asked Kate.

"You'll find out," Kate replied mysteriously.

Chip set off at a trot, leading the others toward the Old Place. Up ahead, Mr. Blake's pickup was parked in the middle of the dirt track just behind the big flatbed truck, which was now empty. At first they could only hear the roar of the bulldozer, but they could see that it had already made a couple of passes through what had been the front yard of the old house. Chip's heart fell when he finally spotted the bulldozer pushing what was left of the house's foundations up in a pile. Heaped in among the dirt and old bricks were hibiscus bushes, their red and pink flowers wilted and crushed. And somewhere in there, Chip knew, was a crushed red-winged blackbird's nest.

Ruben sprinted ahead of the others, raced around the bulldozer, and leapt up on the heap of rubble. He started dancing around on top, making boxing gestures at the bulldozer, like he was going to take it on with his bare fists. It was pretty funny, but also scary. If the bulldozer didn't stop in time, Ruben could get seriously hurt.

Mr. Blake ran toward the bulldozer, yelling and waving at the driver to stop. The blade lifted, then the bulldozer rumbled around the pile and headed for the old barn. Mr. Blake shouted at Ruben, but the boy just laughed. When Mr. Blake climbed up to grab him, Ruben scooted down the other side of the heap.

Ralph and Letoria yelled at Mr. Blake to leave Ruben alone, but Chip, Luther, Lily, Miguel, and Kishan all ran toward the barn. Running alongside the bulldozer's big tracks, they screamed at the driver. He probably couldn't hear anything they were saying, but he did see them. He stopped, turned off the engine, and spit out some very bad words.

Mr. Blake jogged up all out of breath. "Get away from that dozer!" he panted.

The driver called down at him, "How the heck do you

expect me to work with a bunch of maniac kids running all over the place?"

Mr. Blake zeroed in on Chip and Luther. "What do you think you're doing?" he demanded.

"We're protesting," Luther said politely. "We don't want you to tear this place up."

"You're killing the wildlife." Chip tried to keep his voice calm. "We want you to stop."

"You think anything gets built without killing stuff?" snapped Mr. Blake. "That's how it's done. You get rid of what's there, then you build something better."

Lily had climbed up on one of the bulldozer's big metal treads, and she stood looking down at Mr. Blake. "A meat-packing plant isn't better!"

"Who says?" Mr. Blake demanded. "Don't you kids eat meat?"

Nobody answered, because the truth was, all of them except Luther liked meat.

Mr. Blake snorted. "That's what I thought. You don't want to see a meatpacking plant built here, but you sure want your hamburgers and hot dogs and fried chicken, don't you?"

"There are other places," Kishan said. "Places already cleared, where you wouldn't have to destroy so many birds' nests and rabbit burrows."

"Maybe," said Mr. Blake, "but this is *my* place. And I intend to put my plant *here*."

Chip hadn't noticed that Brad had arrived until he spoke up. "Excuse me, sir. I'm a reporter. Is this your property? Or have you just leased it? Do you have permission from the owner to build here?"

Mr. Blake's face turned red. Instead of answering Brad's questions, Mr. Blake grabbed Lily and lifted her off the bulldozer's metal tread. "Get going!" he yelled up to the driver. "Get that barn down!"

But before the driver could restart the engine, a voice came floating down from the loft of the old barn. "Yoo-hoo!"

Everyone looked up. A hand was waving through one of the holes.

"Oh, good grief! There's another kid inside!" Mr. Blake looked over at a couple of workers standing near his pickup. "You two come get this kid out of the loft!" he bellowed.

The men put down their shovels and went inside the barn. All the children crowded in behind them, so now instead of one kid in the barn, there were eleven.

"You want to get killed?" Mr. Blake shouted. "Come down from there!"

"How'd she get up there?" asked one of the men.

"I live here. With the barn owls," said the singsong voice from the loft. "If you push the barn down, you'll destroy our home."

"There's no ladder," a workman said to Mr. Blake. "And no way I can see to climb up without one."

Chip recognized Kate's voice and knew exactly what she'd done. She'd gone up the ladder, then pulled it up after her. He started snickering, then Luther and Lily joined in.

"Okay, forget it," Blake told his men. "Go back to work. She'll come down when we bring in the dozer."

Chip was the last one out of the barn. Lily, Miguel, Kishan, Jesse, Letoria, Ralph, Ruben, and Luther were all sitting in front of the bulldozer blade. Chip walked over and sat down beside them.

Brad took out his camera. "Do you really plan to operate heavy equipment," he asked Mr. Blake, "with all these children around?"

Mr. Blake eyed the row of kids, then looked at Brad with his camera. He muttered a bad word under his breath and called up to the bulldozer driver, "Okay, put 'er back on the truck, Frank. That'll be all for today."

"All right, but I don't work by the hour," Frank called back. "You hire me for the day, you pay me for a day—even if you decide to quit after one hour."

"You'll get paid," Mr. Blake snapped.

"I'm already booked for the next few days," the bulldozer operator added. "Next week is the earliest I can reschedule."

Mr. Blake climbed up on the bulldozer and spoke to the driver in a low, angry voice. The driver nodded and Mr. Blake climbed down. Standing with his hands on his hips, he glared at the kids sitting in front of the blade.

"Well?" he growled. "You want us to leave, so we're leaving. Are you going to get out of the way so we can load the dozer back on the truck, or are you going to sit there like lumps of dirt?"

Miguel got up and walked over to stand by the barn. Chip and the others went to stand beside him, just in case the driver should change his mind and try to push the barn down. But he didn't. He backed the bulldozer up, turned it around, and steered it toward the flatbed truck.

It took awhile for them to load the bulldozer. Chip and the others waited quietly until the truck and Mr. Blake's pickup drove away. Then they jumped up and down, cheered, and generally went crazy at their victory.

Brad went inside the barn to help Kate lower the ladder from the loft so she could come down. Before they could put the ladder away, all the community center kids begged to see the baby barn owls. Chip figured they deserved that for helping to save them.

Lily, meanwhile, tried to get the rabbits to come out, but not one appeared. Chip didn't blame them. The grassy area where they always fed the rabbits had been churned to mud by the bulldozer. They'd probably been terrified by the noise. Chip thought that organizing the protest was probably the most important thing any of them had ever done. He hoped the others felt as proud as he did.

Brad took several pictures of the mess the bulldozer had made, including one of the smashed blackbird's nest. Then he told the kids it was time to get back to school.

Chip was pretty sure they would all get in trouble for being late, but that didn't keep him from being glad they had done it. The only thing that worried him, just a little, was Kate. She hardly said a word on the way back.

When Brad asked her what was the matter, she said, "I don't think this will be the end of it. It was just too easy."

20
A Sudden End

When Chip, Luther, Lily, and the others came trooping into Mr. O'Dell's class two hours late with mud all over their sneakers, all he said was, "Everyone who came in late missed a pop quiz, and I'm not offering a makeup. That zero isn't going to help your grades." At lunch, Ruben, who was in fifth grade, said his teacher gave him a detention because it wasn't the first time he'd been late.

Miguel didn't come out with the rest of the junior high kids after school, so they figured he must have gotten a detention too. None of them knew what happened if you missed your first two periods in seventh grade.

They were standing around on the community center playground, trying to decide whether to start practice or wait for Miguel, when he came running up. He looked excited. Chip couldn't tell if he it was because something good had happened or something terrible. But it was definitely something *big*.

"What? What?" They all crowded around Miguel.

"*Sí, Sí!*" Miguel often went back to speaking in Spanish when he was keyed up.

Chip knew he was saying, "Yes, yes!" But—yes what?

"I was told to report to my homeroom teacher after school,"

Miguel explained. "I thought I was to be punished. Especially when Mrs. Schonberg looked so sad and said she had enjoyed having me in her class and was sorry to see me go. I thought I was to be kicked out of school!" Miguel's face broke into a big, bewildered grin. "Then she asked if I knew where we were being relocated. I did not understand. She explained that they were moving us."

"Moving you?" Lily echoed. "Where to?"

"I do not know. Mrs. Schonberg said she heard it on the news. They have found new homes for us. Tomorrow, she said, will be our last day in this town."

Miguel spoke clearly, but Chip wasn't sure he understood. Was everybody at the community center going to be moved, just like that?

"I think it will be the last day for all of us living here." Miguel waved toward the community center building. "All of us—" He paused, seeming unsure. "Maybe all of us will get real homes."

"Where?" demanded Ruben.

"I don't know. Mrs. Schonberg didn't know either."

Chip glanced around at the faces of the community center kids. They looked confused, like they'd woken up in the middle of a dream and didn't know where they were.

"My dad said the government is buying mobile homes," Jesse said, "and setting them up in different places for people like us to live in."

"Where?" Ralph asked. "Here in Florida?"

Jesse looked uncertain. "Some, I think. And some in other states."

"I hated it when I first came here," said Letoria, sounding close to tears. "But now I've got friends. I don't want to move again!"

"I didn't want to move the first time," said Ruben. "But who ever asked us? Not the hurricane, that's for sure!"

"Our parents must know," said Kishan. "I'm going to ask." She and several of the others took off running toward the community center building.

Chip, Luther, and Lily had remained quiet up till then. They were as shocked as everybody else. And like everybody else, they didn't fully understand what was about to happen.

It was Luther who spoke first. "I wish all of you could stay!"

"Yeah," said Chip. "Maybe the places they found for you are right around here!"

"You've *got* to stay!" Lily cried, looking at Miguel. "We're just getting it together as a team! By next year we'd be awesome! We could field a junior high team good enough to beat the high school team!"

Chip knew that was a major exaggeration, but they did play well as a group. Or *had* played well. But now it seemed like the community center team was about to be history.

"They don't have a choice," Luther reminded Lily.

"Even if they did, they need a home more than a soccer team."

Lily turned her big black eyes on Chip and, to his amazement, he saw that they were filled with tears. In the four years since he'd met Lily, he had never once seen her cry. Lily just got mad. Now it looked like she was going to be mad and cry at the same time.

Miguel must have seen it too. "You must not cry yet," he said softly to Lily. "We do not know what will happen. Especially to me. My mother and I, we are not citizens. We may not be given a place to live in your country. Or maybe we will, and it will be nearby."

"What about a game this afternoon anyway?" Lily asked, blinking back the tears.

Glancing around, Chip saw that there weren't enough kids left on the field to make up even one team, let alone two.

Miguel shook his head sadly. "No, *amiga*. I think we have played our last game together."

The few remaining kids said goodbye and followed Miguel into the building.

Chip glanced at Lily. She was hugging her soccer ball like it was the only friend in the world she had left.

"How can something you've worked so hard at end just like that?" she asked.

It started to rain before they got home. "At least the rain is keeping the ground soggy, so it'll be harder for Mr. Blake to come back," Chip said, trying to recover the good feeling they'd had after the protest. "I wonder how the rabbits are doing?"

"Better than they'd be if we'd let Mr. Blake's bulldozer squash their burrows," Lily said as she veered off into the nursery parking lot.

Chip and Luther crossed the highway to Lost Goat Lane, and without even discussing the matter, headed for Luther's house. They'd just stepped up onto the Wilsons' porch when Ruby came bursting out. "Oh, Luther! And Chip! Will you boys see if you can get that darn goat out of the garden?"

Chip looked toward the garden and saw a white goat browsing on Mrs. Wilson's vegetables. It wasn't Old Billy. It was a smaller goat, without horns.

"Where'd that one come from?" Chip asked as they jogged out to the garden.

"The owner brought her out yesterday to marry Old Billy." Luther grinned and added, "You know what I mean."

Chip snickered. It meant a neighbor had brought the goat out to be bred by Old Billy, in hopes that the babies would be prizewinners like him. Mrs. Wilson always referred to it as the goats "getting married," which made Chip and Luther laugh.

Chip said, "If goats really did have weddings, I guess Old Billy would have about a hundred wives by now."

The white goat watched as they walked toward her. Then she started leaping back and forth across the garden, trampling squash vines underfoot and knocking down pole beans. They chased her out of the vegetables and cornered her in the flower bed next to the house. Seeing that she could not escape, she bit off a large pink rose and stood chewing on it, thorns and all.

Chip and Luther grabbed her collar and dragged her back to the goat pasture.

Then they went into the house to let Ruby know the bride goat was back where she belonged. Mrs. Wilson was sitting on the sofa with one leg up, an ice pack propped on her knee.

"What happened to your leg, Grandma?" Luther asked.

"That silly goat!" Mrs. Wilson exclaimed. "I guess she was none too happy about being married off to Old Billy. She kept bleating all morning long. I thought if I took her a little treat, she might hush, so I carried a pan of potato peelings out to the pen. I'd just opened the gate to go in when she came barreling past me like she was being chased by the devil. Knocked me clean over! And this old knee—" Mrs. Wilson shifted positions and winced a little.

"Shouldn't you go to the doctor?" Luther asked.

"Well, now, I don't think it's that bad," Mrs. Wilson said.

"But your mama has already called Mr. Jackson to come drive us to town, so I guess that's what we're going to do."

"Better safe than sorry," Ruby called from the kitchen.

Just then Mr. Jackson's car pulled up out front. Ruby held the door open while Chip and Luther helped Mrs. Wilson up from the couch and slowly walked her out onto the porch. Mrs. Wilson leaned heavily on Chip, who was on the side with the injured leg. Luther held on to her other arm and kept an umbrella over her head to keep the rain off. They walked down Booker's wheelchair ramp so she wouldn't have to bend her bad leg. Then Chip heard Ruby say to Richard, "Mama and Papa should think about moving into town. This place is getting to be too much for them."

Mrs. Wilson stopped in her tracks and asked in a low voice, "Did you boys hear that?"

"Yes'm," Chip mumbled.

Luther didn't say anything, but he looked upset.

"People who think they know what's best for other people are often overstepping their bounds." Mrs. Wilson paused and gave them a sly grin. "So let's pretend we never heard that. You ignore a silly notion, it'll generally go away."

Luther's face broke into a relieved grin. "Yes, ma'am!"

Mrs. Wilson, muttering about old bones, eased herself into Mr. Jackson's car. Chip took the umbrella so Luther could help her find the end of the seat belt and get it fastened.

"Thanks, boys," Mr. Jackson said, and gave them a thumbs-up as he slid behind the wheel of the car. "You've done your good deed for the day."

"Their second good deed," Ruby said from the backseat. "Their first one was getting that goat out of the garden."

As the car drove away, Chip said to Luther, "Our *third* good deed of the day. Getting rid of Blake's gang was number one."

"Yeah," Luther said. But the frown on his face told Chip he was thinking about something else. "You ever notice how little my grandma's getting?" Luther asked.

Chip laughed. "She's the same size she always was, Luther. We're just getting bigger."

21

House Arrest

If Tuesday had been the most exciting day of the week—with the protest and news that the community center kids were finally going to get real homes—Wednesday was the most boring. None of the kids from the center came to school, which made the classroom and the table where they usually sat in the lunchroom feel empty. Nobody knew whether they had already been taken to their new homes or were waiting to find out where they were being sent.

Chip, Luther, and Lily rode the bus home in glum silence. Lily had planned to go to the community center after school to see what was going on, but it was still raining. As the bus rolled past the center playground, Chip couldn't see anyone. He glanced over at Lily. She looked more depressed than ever.

When the bus passed the apartment building where Mr. Jackson lived, Luther turned away from the window. Chip figured he had gone back to being mad about his mother's plan for them to live there.

Chip would have tried to cheer up his friends, but he had worries too. He kept thinking about what Kate had said after the protest: *I don't think this will be the end of it. It was just too easy.*

Chip remembered the bulldozer driver telling Mr. Blake he'd be available again next week. What if Blake brought the bulldozer back then? How many times could they skip school to protest? And what good would it do? There were only three of them now.

Then Chip thought about Brad's article. It was due out tomorrow, in Thursday's paper. Surely that would make a difference.

Brad's article did come out the following day, and it definitely made a difference. But in his worst nightmares, Chip could not have imagined what it would be.

The first hint of trouble came after lunch on Thursday. Mr. O'Dell called Chip, Luther, and Lily up to his desk and said in a low, worried voice, "Each of your parents left a message. They said you're to come directly home on the bus after school. They didn't say why."

Lily stalked back to her desk. She was furious because she'd been planning to go to the community center after school to see if any of their friends were still around.

"What do you think?" Luther whispered as they returned to their seats.

"Probably something to do with the protest," Chip muttered. "But we only missed a couple of hours of school. Can't be that bad."

He figured their punishment wouldn't be more than a week or two without TV. So what? In the Jungle, they had something better than TV to watch anyway.

It wasn't until Chip saw Ruby waiting at the bus stop that he realized they might be in serious trouble. Her face—no, her entire body—looked hopping mad. She didn't even wait till the bus pulled away to start in on Luther.

"You!" she raged at him in a voice so shrill that every kid on the bus heard her. "I ought to ground you for life!"

"What?" Luther asked, his face screwed up with a mixture of fear and embarrassment.

As the bus drove off, Chip saw Mom and Mr. Hashimoto crossing the highway from the nursery. By the hard, fast way they were walking, he could tell they were just as mad as Ruby.

"Chip Martin!" Mom yelled. "You go straight to the house and don't set foot outside except to do your chores, do you hear me? You'd better have every speck of your homework done when I get there too."

"What, Mom?" Chip asked. "What've we done?"

"What have you *done*?" Mr. Hashimoto jerked a folded newspaper out from under his arm, whipped it open, and stuck it under Lily's nose. "That's what I'd like to know! No, not *what* have you done—the whole town knows that! What I want to know is *why*?"

Lily stared down at the newspaper. Chip and Luther peered over her shoulder. What they saw was a large picture of themselves and the community center kids lined up in front of Mr. Blake's bulldozer. The bold headline said "Local Kids Stop Construction."

Chip swelled with pride, but only for a nanosecond. Then he read the small headline under the big one: "Builder May Sue to Recover Costs." As that sentence sunk in, he felt himself shrinking down to the size of one very scared kid.

Just then two cars pulled into the nursery parking lot.

"Customers, Betty," Mr. Hashimoto said to Chip's mom. "We'll have to deal with this later." To Lily he said, "Daughter, go home and explain yourself to your mother. She is so upset she has gone to bed with a sick headache!"

"Shall we meet at my place after work and try to get to the bottom of this?" Chip's mom asked.

Mr. Hashimoto had already started back across the highway. "Good idea," he said over his shoulder.

"I'm definitely going to get to the bottom of it," Ruby said. "And when I do—!" She gave Luther a look that made Chip glad she wasn't *his* mom.

Chip trudged up the driveway to his house alone. He wished he'd had a chance to read the whole article. The word that stuck in his mind—and sat there flashing like a neon light—was *sue*. He knew people sued other people for millions of dollars for all kinds of things. Could Mr. Blake really sue Mom and the Wilsons and the Hashimotos for a lot of money just because their kids had stopped his stupid construction project?

As soon as he got into the house, Chip fell down on the couch and lay there with his face buried in the cushions.

He heard a car drive up, followed by excited voices coming toward the house, then Kate and Brad burst through the door. Chip felt like punching Brad for all the trouble his article had caused.

"Chip, have you seen it?" Brad shouted, waving a newspaper.

"It's a *great* article!" Kate exulted. "Oh, Chip, wait till you—" She stopped in midsentence. "What's the matter? Are you sick?"

"No," Chip said. "I am not sick. And I already saw the article. So did Mom and the Wilsons and the Hashimotos. And they do not think it's so great that we're going to get *sued*." Chip gave Brad an accusing look. "Why did you write that?

And right on top of the page too!"

Brad glanced at Kate, his excitement waning. "I didn't write that part," he said. "They have special people at the paper who write the headlines. I only wrote the article. Didn't you like it?"

"I never got that far," Chip said. "I don't think Mom and Ruby did either. Everybody got stuck on that word *sue*."

Brad knelt down next to the sofa and stuck a copy of the paper in Chip's hand. "Read the article. It explains everything. And inside, see, they used two of my pictures. Three, counting the big one on the first page. It's a major story, Chip. For this little town, really huge!"

"Great," Chip said flatly and started reading. Actually it *was* a good article. There were quotes from Chip, Luther, Lily, and some of the other kids about how they were trying to protect the homes of the animals that lived on the land and how much they'd enjoyed going there on a field trip. There was even a quote from Mr. O'Dell explaining how important it was to keep some areas in native vegetation to provide habitat for wild animals. The two pictures Brad had mentioned were of Luther scratching Miz Rabbit's ears and Lily looking into the nest of a red-winged blackbird.

The last sentence in the article said that the owner was in a nursing home and possibly was not aware of Mr. Blake's intentions to build a meatpacking plant there. Then it said, in small print, "See follow-up story in Monday edition."

"What does that mean?" Chip asked.

"Mr. Pyper—he's the editor—asked me to do a follow-up," Brad explained excitedly. "For Monday's paper. A rebuttal to the piece on Mr. Blake."

"What piece on Mr. Blake? And what's a rebuttal?" Chip asked.

"Here." Brad pointed to a short article next to the one about the protest. "After the editor read my piece, he sent another reporter to interview Mr. Blake. He's the one who reported that Mr. Blake might sue the parents of the kids involved."

"He's going to have a hard time finding most of them," Chip said with grim satisfaction. "All the community center kids have left—or will be leaving soon. Anyway, Blake doesn't even know who they are."

"Listen, Chip." Kate sat down cross-legged on the carpet next to Brad. "Blake's not going to sue anybody. He admitted to Mr. O'Dell that he more or less tricked old Mrs. Franklin into leasing the place to him. There's a good chance that what he's trying to do is illegal. We've already started checking into it."

"Mr. Pyper wants proof," Kate added. "He owns the newspaper, and if he prints something that turns out not to be true, *he* could get sued."

"I'm sure I can get proof," Brad said. "Well, pretty sure."

Chip flopped back on the couch and stared at the ceiling. "I hope you find it before Mom gets home. Because when she does…" He didn't bother to finish the sentence. Kate and Brad knew, just like Chip knew, that the worse kind of trouble a kid can get in is the kind that gets his parents in trouble too.

After Brad left, Kate tried three times to call Ruby, but the line was busy. Chip did his homework, then helped Kate fix supper.

When Mom got home, they sat down to supper like always, but nobody seemed to feel like talking. Mom only spoke twice, once to ask Kate to bring more milk from the fridge and once to ask Chip if he'd finished his homework.

Mom's silence made Chip so nervous that he couldn't eat. Finally he asked, "When are people coming over?"

"Not tonight," Mom said wearily. "Mrs. Hashimoto isn't feeling well, and Ruby wants to consult a lawyer first. We rescheduled the meeting for tomorrow night."

Chip could see how upset Mom was. Her face was pale and even her hair, which was about the same blonde as Kate's, seemed kind of grayish. He felt terrible knowing that her tired, strained look was on account of him. He wished he could do something to make her feel better, but what could he do when *he* was the problem? Disappear?

Kate must have been trying to think of something to cheer Mom up too, because she said brightly, "You know, Mom, I think Mr. Blake is just bluffing. Brad says—"

"I frankly don't want to hear what Brad has to say!" Mom interrupted sharply. "It's what *he said* that blew this mess all out of proportion! Just to get his name in the paper!"

"No, Mom!" Chip exclaimed. "That's not the reason why—"

"Of course not!" Mom practically shouted. *"You* are the reason why! Brad only made it worse by blabbing to the press!"

"Mom!" Kate cried in exasperation. "Get a grip! *You're* the one who's blowing it all out of proportion."

"Oh, am I?" Mom's voice turned icy cold. "Well, take a look at *this*, young lady!"

Mom pulled a folded envelope out of her jeans pocket and slapped it on the table between Kate and Chip. "Read *that*. And then tell me I'm exaggerating about this…this—" She looked at Chip and burst into tears.

Chip reached across the table to touch his mother's hand and say he was sorry, but she ran into the bathroom and slammed the door behind her.

Kate picked up the envelope and pulled out the letter. Chip looked at it over her shoulder.

"It's from a lawyer," Kate whispered, as if Chip couldn't see that for himself. "He says his client Mr. Blake wants five thousand dollars in damages."

"What for?" asked Chip, who was trying to read, listen to Kate, and understand the meaning of the lawyer's big words all at the same time.

"It says, 'for your minor son's participation in the blockage of a legitimate construction project.'"

"Meaning me?"

"Meaning you," Kate said. "I guess he didn't mention me because he never actually saw me."

"He knows where Luther lives. And probably Lily too, since they're the only Japanese American family around."

"Then the Wilsons and Hashimotos probably got one of these too," Kate said, putting the letter back in the envelope.

"Are we going to have to pay him?" Chip asked.

Kate narrowed her blue eyes and stared hard at the envelope. "I don't know, Chip. But one thing I'm pretty sure of: If Blake's construction project isn't legal in the first place, then he probably can't sue anybody for stopping it."

Kate carried the dishes to the sink and began to wash them. Chip was wiping the table when Mom came out of the bathroom. Without speaking to either of them, she went into the living room and picked up the telephone.

Chip and Kate stood still for a minute, to hear who she was talking to.

"Booker," Kate whispered.

Usually when Mom talked to Booker, she laughed a lot. Not tonight, though. Tonight she was crying.

22

Zones, Permits, and Variances

Friday felt like the longest school day of the year. During math, Chip kept making mistakes because the only number that would stick in his head was five thousand. During English, Mr. O'Dell assigned them a one-page essay called "What I Worry About." While the other kids wrote, Chip doodled. He was worried about so many things he didn't know where to start.

Chip only got three sentences down before the bell rang: "Sometimes I worry about bad things that might happen, but then they don't happen. Sometimes bad things happen that I never thought to worry about. The trouble is, you never can tell which bad things are really going to happen, so you don't know which ones you should worry about."

At lunch Chip sat with Luther and Lily, away from the other kids. None of the community center kids had come to school again. The buzz was that some families had already been taken to their new homes and the rest were leaving today. Nobody seemed to know for sure.

"There was probably something about it on the news," Luther said. "But I didn't get to watch because I had to stay in my room."

"I'll go find out this afternoon," Lily said.

Chip was surprised. "Aren't you grounded?"

"So what?" Lily said, sounding almost as rebellious as Ruben.

"How long do you think we'll be under house arrest?" Chip asked.

"Till we go away to college," Luther said glumly.

"Unless we can prove that Mr. Blake doesn't have a building permit. Then *he'd* get in trouble instead of us," Chip said.

"How can we find that out?" Lily asked.

Chip shrugged. "Maybe look on the Internet?"

"Look for what?" Luther asked.

"I don't know," Chip said crankily, wondering why they were aiming questions at him like he was supposed to have all the answers.

The moment lunch period was over, they hurried back to their classroom. Luther and Lily immediately sat down at the two vacant computers. "Try Googling *building permits* for this county," Chip suggested.

About a zillion links came on the screen. It was impossible to tell which one had what they were looking for, because they didn't really know *what* they were looking for. Mr. O'Dell walked up behind them to see what they were doing. For a minute he didn't say anything, just watched Luther and Lily clicking on one link after another. "Are you trying to find out how the Old Place is zoned?" he asked.

"Yes sir," Chip said.

"Land out there is probably zoned agricultural, for farming. Except right along the highway. The land that fronts on the highway may be zoned commercial."

Luther turned around in his chair. "Does that mean Mr. Blake couldn't get a permit to build a meatpacking plant unless it was on the highway?"

"Actually, a meatpacking plant isn't commercial," Mr. O'Dell said. "It's industrial. I expect he'd have to get a variance."

"A variance?" Chip, Luther, and Lily repeated together.

"That's permission for a person build something in an area where the zoning normally doesn't allow it," Mr. O'Dell explained. "I had to get a variance when I wanted to build a greenhouse in my backyard."

"Who gives a variance?" Chip asked.

"The local variance committee," Mr. O'Dell explained. "The builder has to show the committee members his plans. Usually they contact the neighbors to see if it's okay with them. My neighbors didn't object to a greenhouse, so I got a variance to build it."

"Would it be in the phone book? Like under *V*?" Chip asked.

Mr. O'Dell shook his head. "I don't think so. I had to take my plans down to the courthouse, and, well, I don't remember for sure what the process was. If you want me to, I'll find out and let you know on Monday."

Luther and Lily logged off without saying anything. They all knew Monday would be too late.

Suddenly a thought hit Chip. "Wait, did you say they give out permits and variances at the courthouse?"

"That's where you apply," Mr. O'Dell said. "But it would be the county commissioners, or the variance committee members, who make the actual decision."

"Mr. O'Dell, I just remembered something I gotta tell my sister!" Chip said breathlessly. "She's in the cafeteria now, so can I—I mean, I know the bell already rang—but can I go if I hurry?"

"Are you sure—?" Mr. O'Dell began.

"Yes sir! It's really, really important!" Chip exclaimed. "I'll be right back!"

Without waiting for an answer, he grabbed a pass from Mr. O'Dell's desk and tore out of the room. He headed across the parking lot toward the high school cafeteria where Kate would be having lunch.

Except she wasn't. When he was halfway across the parking lot he saw her standing on the front steps of the high school, staring up the street. Chip changed directions and ran over to her.

She frowned as he dashed up. "What're you doing out here, Chip?"

"What're *you* doing here? I thought you'd be having lunch."

"Looking for Brad," Kate said. "He went down to the courthouse to see if—oh, here he comes now!"

Chip turned and saw Brad's SUV pull into the parking lot. Kate hurried over to meet him. Chip followed.

"Any luck?" she called as Brad got out.

"Not much." Brad looked discouraged. "I did see a map that shows that all the land around the Old Place is zoned agricultural. And I found a list of the county commissioners. I tried phoning them but only managed to get hold of two people."

"Come on, tell us!" Kate was almost shouting at him. "What did they say?"

Brad sighed. "One guy said he didn't recall anything about a building permit being issued for a meatpacking plant, and the other one, when I said I was working on an article, said he didn't want to discuss zoning decisions with the press."

"So does that mean yes or no?" Chip asked.

Kate looked around at Chip, as if just remembering he was there. "What are you doing out of class?"

"I came to see if you can go to the courthouse and find out about variances."

"Variances?" Kate and Brad repeated together, just the way Chip, Luther, and Lily had when they first heard it.

Chip explained what Mr. O'Dell had told them. "So Brad, can you go back to the courthouse and find out if Mr. Blake got a variance to build a meatpacking plant out there?"

Brad looked at his watch. "Can't. Math test next period. In fact, I gotta run." He shouldered his book bag and glanced at Kate to see if she was coming. But she motioned for him to go on without her.

Then she said to Chip, "I'll go. I think I can find out more than Brad did."

"Really? How?"

"He might not've asked the right people."

"Like who?"

"Clerks at the courthouse. Secretaries." Kate grinned. "They do most of the actual work, so they'd be the ones who know what's really going on." She patted Chip on the shoulder. "You better go back now."

"What about your classes?"

"Don't worry about me." Kate gave him a smug grin. "*I'm* an A student, and A students get privileges."

She started off across the parking lot, then turned and called back, "And Chip, stop worrying!"

Chip waved, then jogged slowly back to his classroom. He'd be glad to stop worrying, if he only knew how.

23
Backup

Kate wasn't on the bus that afternoon. Neither was Lily. Chip watched out the window as the bus turned onto the street that went past the community center. Sure enough, there was Lily, striding along the sidewalk with a soccer ball under her arm.

"Oh boy," Luther muttered. "She's really going to catch it when she gets home."

After a couple of blocks, Chip said, "And she's doing it all for nothing. Look." People holding bundles and babies were lined up in front of the community center, waiting their turn to get onto a big bus.

"Yeah," Luther said. "By the time she gets there, they'll all be gone."

The house was empty when Chip got home. He guessed Kate had missed the bus because she was still at the courthouse, but as the afternoon wore on he began to worry all over again. Surely the courthouse had closed by now.

Mom had left a meatloaf out to thaw for dinner. Chip put it and three baking potatoes in the oven, then went out to feed the ducks. He milked the goats, even though it was Kate's shift. He'd just come in from doing the chores when the phone rang.

"Chip," Kate said breathlessly. "Will you do the milking for me tonight?"

"Already did," Chip said. "Where are you?"

"With Brad," Kate said. "Look, I won't be home for supper. Tell Mom we're working on a project. I'll come as soon as I can."

"How soon?" Chip asked, glancing at the clock. "The meeting's at seven."

"We'll try to make it," Kate said.

"Don't *try*," Chip said. *"Be here!"*

But Kate had already hung up.

Chip stared at the dead phone, feeling a twinge of panic at the thought that Kate might not get home in time for the grown-ups' meeting. Then he spotted Justin's Atlanta phone number right in front of his face on a list of emergency numbers. He punched in the number, not knowing what he was going to say. He just wanted to hear his brother's voice.

"Kevin speaking!" barked a voice that wasn't Justin's.

"Can I speak to Justin, please?"

"He's not here!" Kevin yelled over the loud music in the background.

"Do you know when he'll be back?" Chip asked.

"Gone for the weekend!" Kevin shouted. "Wanna leave a message?"

"No thanks." Chip hung up, wondering where Justin might have gone for the weekend.

He heard a car door slam and looked out the window. For a minute he thought he was having a hallucination. There was his brother, walking up the driveway! Justin ran the last few yards, skipped up the steps, and flung open the door.

"Hi," he said, barging through the living room and down the hall. He shrugged off his backpack, tossed it into the bedroom, and came back to where Chip was standing with his mouth open.

"Hi." Chip closed his mouth, but he was still in a state of shock. "What're you doing here?"

"I heard you kids got your tails caught in a crack." Justin grinned. "Or that's what Booker said, who got it from Mom." Justin put an arm around Chip's shoulder. "So what's the story, bro?"

Chip felt like crying, which would have made no sense at all, because he was really *glad* Justin was there. He swallowed the lump in his throat and explained the situation.

"I've got five thousand dollars," Justin said when Chip had finished.

"You?" Chip asked in amazement.

"My college fund," Justin said. "We could use that if we had to."

"That's crazy!" Chip exclaimed. "Mom wouldn't let you anyway." Chip was beginning to realize that as bad as things were right now, they could get a lot worse. If Justin had to use his money to pay Blake, he'd have to drop out of college, and it would all be Chip's fault.

"Is that why you came home?" Chip asked, feeling guilty. "To tell Mom she could have your college money to fix this mess?"

"Naw. I could've told her that on the phone. I thought you might need a little backup, that's all." Justin headed for the kitchen. "Where's Kate?"

Chip didn't get a chance to answer because at that moment Mom walked in.

"Justin!" She gave him a big hug. "I thought you might

want to come down with Booker. But won't missing a day of classes be a problem?"

"Not really. I only have two classes on Fridays." Justin poured himself a glass of milk. "Anyway, college isn't like high school. Most professors don't mind an occasional absence as long as you do the work."

While Mom washed her hands, Chip took the potatoes and meatloaf out of the oven and put them on the table, then tossed together a quick salad. Mom didn't even look at him until they sat down. "Where's Kate?" she asked.

"Working on a school project," Chip said, even though Kate hadn't said it was a *school* project. Hopefully it was a completely different kind of project.

Mom's lips tightened. "You kids are starting to run wild. Coming and going as you please without even bothering to ask permission."

"She...she's not running wild," Chip stammered. "She'll be home pretty soon."

Fortunately for Chip, Justin kept up a patter of small talk about his classes and his new college friends. Mom listened, but Chip could tell she was waiting for the sound of Brad's SUV bringing Kate home.

So was he.

Seven o'clock came and Kate still wasn't home. Booker arrived first, with Mr. and Mrs. Wilson and Luther. While Chip was helping Luther lift Booker's wheelchair up the porch steps, the Hashimotos pulled into the driveway. Chip wondered why they drove when they lived so close, until he saw Mrs. Hashimoto. She was pale and slumped over, like she didn't feel well enough to be out of bed. Lily trailed behind her parents, looking almost as pale as her mother. Chip wondered how much more trouble she had gotten into for going to the community center instead of coming straight home on the bus.

Then Mr. Jackson's car pulled into the driveway. Ruby was with him.

"What's he here for?" Chip asked Luther under his breath.

"Same reason Uncle Booker's here," Luther muttered. "Our moms figure we're so bad they've got to have backup."

"Well, at least we have Justin for our backup," Chip said, his throat tightening again. He couldn't believe his brother had come all the way from Atlanta just because he heard they were in trouble.

"What happened to Kate?" asked Luther. "I thought she—"

"Who knows?" Chip said.

Mom gave Mr. and Mrs. Hashimoto the two armchairs. Mrs. Hashimoto in her blue kimono was practically swallowed by the big easy chair. She scooted to one side and motioned for Lily to sit next to her. Lily pretended not to notice and sat cross-legged on the floor in front of the TV.

Mr. and Mrs. Wilson and Ruby lined up on the sofa, with Luther squished in the middle. Booker wheeled his chair to one end of the sofa, and Mom brought out two kitchen chairs, one for her and one for Mr. Jackson.

Chip sat down by Lily and signaled with his eyes for Luther to join them. Luther quickly moved onto the floor next to Chip. The eight adults looked like people staring at a TV program they didn't much like. Chip and Luther and Lily were the whole show.

Justin stood in the doorway between the kitchen and living room, not one of the kids anymore, but not exactly one of the grown-ups either.

"I guess," said Mr. Hashimoto slowly, "we may as well start

with this." He held up the letter from Mr. Blake's lawyer. "I suppose you know that the developer is demanding five thousand dollars from each of us to cover the expenses he incurred when you children blocked his construction project." Nobody said anything, so Mr. Hashimoto went on. "If we don't pay the damages he is claiming, he will take us to court. If it goes to court, we will have to hire lawyers. If we lose, it would end up costing us even more."

"Mr. Hashimoto," Ruby said. "Richard has a friend who's an attorney. We spoke with him today." She touched Mr. Jackson's arm. "Richard, why don't you tell them what he said?"

Mr. Jackson sat up straight, hands on his knees, and cleared his throat. "I realize this is not my affair, but as Ruby's fiancé, I naturally want to help in any way I can."

"And we all appreciate your help, Richard," Mom said. "Did your lawyer friend have any suggestions?"

"Basically he said that if the developer has a permit to build there, he probably can collect damages. The five thousand dollars he is claiming from each of you is probably far more than the delay actually cost him, but as Mr. Hashimoto pointed out, if you go to court to fight it, it could end up costing that much or more."

"Is that it?" Mom asked.

"That's it," Richard said. "*If* the guy has a permit. But my friend said that around here, builders often start construction before the permit is issued. If Blake started work without a permit, then he doesn't have a leg to stand on, because *he* was the one in violation of the law."

"Why would a builder take such a chance?" Mr. Hashimoto asked.

"Well, in a case like this, when a builder knows that construction might be opposed by neighbors, he sometimes goes ahead with the project and waits to apply for a permit. Once work is underway, he can argue that any delay will cause him a big financial loss."

Chip wished Mr. Jackson would get to the point. He just wanted to know if Mr. Blake could sue them or not.

"Developers know," Mr. Jackson continued, "that counties and cities like to issue permits, because more buildings mean more taxes. My friend said that about the only thing that would stop these county commissioners from issuing a building permit is strong protest from the neighbors. Even then, they sometimes give the go-ahead. Especially if construction is already started."

There was silence for a minute, then Mr. Wilson spoke up. "I called the county office when I first heard what this Blake fellow was up to. The lady I talked to said she hadn't heard about any construction out this way."

Mom said, "I called too. The clerk took my number and said somebody would get back to me, but nobody did."

"I spoke to a county commissioner," Mr. Hashimoto said. "He promised to check on the status of the project and let me know, but I haven't heard from him yet."

Booker, who had been unusually quiet, said, "You all have a feeling you're getting the runaround? Like maybe these kids' protest is the only thing that stopped Blake from putting up his meatpacking plant before the neighbors got wind of it?"

Heads nodded. For the first time since the newspaper article had come out, Chip felt a little bit hopeful.

Then Mrs. Hashimoto spoke up. "Naturally we don't want a meatpacking plant out here. But I don't want my Lily involved in something illegal. I *told* my husband that she shouldn't be hanging around with those community center children. They are so—" She paused, searching for the right word. "—so rough-looking! I knew they'd lead her—"

166

"No!" Lily shouted, leaping to her feet. "I told you, Mother. *We* led *them!*"

Chip stood up beside her. "The protest was our idea, Mrs. Hashimoto."

Luther got to his feet too. "*I* asked them if they'd protest with us," he said, sounding scared but also proud. "And they did, because they're our friends."

"Most of them went to the Old Place on our class field trip," Chip explained. "They didn't want the birds' nests and rabbit burrows crushed by Mr. Blake's bulldozer either."

There was another long silence after that. Then Mrs. Wilson said with a heavy sigh, "None of us want to see that place torn up. But it doesn't belong to us."

"It doesn't belong to Mr. Blake either!" Luther shouted. "He *lied* to Mrs. Franklin. He promised her he'd take care of the place. And he *laughed* when he told us, because she's in a nursing home and he said she'd never know."

Mr. Wilson shook his head sadly. "We got rights over our own property, but we got no say about what happens on Mrs. Franklin's land. That's between him and her."

Just then they all heard a vehicle pulling into the driveway.

24

Cat Out of the Bag

hip's mother jumped up and opened the door. "Kate Martin, where have you *been?*" she demanded. As Brad started to come in, she blocked his way. "Brad, I'm afraid I can't invite you in. We're trying to deal with an important matter. The last thing we need is you putting what we say in private in the paper!"

"Mo-om!" Kate protested. "Brad *knows* what's going on. That's where we've been. Getting information." Before Mom could answer, Kate practically yelled to the others in the room, "Mr. Blake does *not* have a building permit!"

There was a babble of voices while everybody tried to talk at once. Mom sighed and stepped aside. "All right, Brad. Come on in. Let's hear what you have to say."

Brad looked nervous, but he seemed to relax a little when Kate took his hand. "Go ahead, Brad," she said. "Tell them what you found out."

Brad pushed the hair out of his eyes and coughed twice. "Um, actually," he began, "it's what Kate found out. I mean, I found out that the Old Place is zoned agricultural. But it was Kate who—"

"Actually," Kate interrupted, "it was Chip who found out Blake had to have a variance before he could get permission to build a meatpacking plant. So *I* went to the courthouse and asked the clerk if he had one. She said Mr. Blake had applied for it but the committee hadn't met yet to decide!"

"Does that mean he can't sue us?" Chip blurted out.

"Looks like it," Mr. Jackson said. "Brad, you and Kate seem to have done an excellent job at getting to the bottom of all this."

"That certainly casts a new light on things," said Mr. Hashimoto.

Ruby turned to Richard. "Would you check with the lawyer one more time? Just to be sure that man doesn't have any grounds for a lawsuit."

"Good idea," Mr. Hashimoto agreed. There were murmurs of agreement and thanks all around the room.

Mr. Jackson nodded, then jotted a few notes on a card and stuck it in his pocket.

Then Justin spoke for the first time. "If nobody does anything else to stop this, I guess the permit will get approved and the builder will go ahead."

"But what can we do?" Mrs. Hashimoto squeezed her tiny hands tightly together. "We are ordinary citizens—not activists."

"*I'm* an activist!" Lily announced.

"Me too," Luther and Chip echoed together.

Booker chuckled. "I think everybody knows that by now."

"The thing is," Chip said, "kids by themselves don't count. We need grown-ups to help us save the Old Place."

Mrs. Wilson shook her head slowly from side to side. "Old folks like us don't count much more than children. Nobody pays us any mind."

"And I have a business to run," said Mr. Hashimoto.

Chip glanced at Luther and Lily. He could tell they were

picking up the same vibes he was: all the adults cared about was not having to pay Mr. Blake a lot of money. Now that they were pretty sure he couldn't sue them, they were satisfied. They might complain about a meatpacking plant being built, but none of them wanted to do anything to stop it.

Chip felt anger welling up in him. The adults were sitting there like frogs on logs, making croaking noises every once in a while, but not willing to stand up for their rights or the rights of wildlife—or even for poor old Mrs. Franklin. He could only think of one thing that might change their minds. It scared him to do it, but he knew he had to.

"We've got to stop Mr. Blake from destroying the Old Place," he said. "Because it's not just rabbits and birds that live there. There's also Florida panthers."

The eight grown-ups stared at him. Justin laughed like it was the craziest thing he had ever heard.

"We've seen them," Luther said.

Booker laughed too, but not in his usual, feel-good way. "Boys, there's a time and place for tall tales, and this is not it."

"It's not a tall tale!" Lily cried. "I've seen them too!"

Kate said, "I almost touched one!"

"Enough!" Ruby said sharply. "I don't know where you kids got the idea that you could get us to believe such a cooked-up piece of nonsense, but I'm warning you, Luther—" She pointed her finger toward him the way she had at the bus stop.

Instead of hanging his head in embarrassment, Luther walked right up to her. "It isn't nonsense, Mom," he said. "I took pictures of them."

"Where?" Ruby demanded. "I haven't seen any."

"They're still at the drugstore. They're ready, but I had to wait until I got my allowance to pick them up."

"Which drugstore?" Mrs. Wilson asked.

"The one down the block from the community center," Luther said.

"It's open till nine," Kate said excitedly. "We can go get them right now!"

Luther suddenly looked scared. "But they might not have turned out."

"They *better* have turned out," Ruby warned. "If you aren't telling the truth—"

"He *is!*" Kate exclaimed. "Come on!" She grabbed Luther by one hand and Brad by the other and they dashed out.

Mom asked if anybody wanted iced tea. Everybody said yes, and Booker wheeled into the kitchen to help her. While they were drinking tea, the Hashimotos and the Wilsons gathered around Mr. Jackson, asking him questions about the meeting with the lawyer.

"I saw you walking to the community center," Chip said to Lily. "Too bad there wasn't time for one more soccer game."

"I didn't go to play soccer," Lily said. "I went to say good-bye to Miguel."

"Did you see him?"

"Yes," Lily said. "He was already on the bus when I got there, but he leaned out of the window and we got to talk for a minute."

"Where was he going?"

"South Bay for now. After that, he doesn't know. He promised to write though."

"I hope he finds somebody to play soccer with," Luther said.

Lily grinned. "He will," she said. "I gave him my soccer ball."

Brad, Kate, and Luther were gone about fifteen minutes. The instant they burst into the house Chip knew that some of the pictures had turned out, because they were all smiling. Without saying a word, Luther started handing out pictures, one to each adult. Chip went to see the one Mom was studying. To his disappointment it was just the blurry rear end of a kitten. It could have been any kind of cat, or even some other animal, dashing into the woods.

The one he gave the Hashimotos must have been a better view. "Why, they're just tiny kittens," Mrs. Hashimoto said. "I thought a panther was a large animal, like a tiger!"

Richard Jackson and Ruby stared in amazement at the snapshot Luther had given them. "What kind of camera did you use, Luther?" Mr. Jackson asked.

"The little Olympus Mama gave me, after you got her that new digital," Luther said.

"It's very difficult to get a good picture of animals in the wild," Mr. Jackson said. "It takes a *lot* of patience."

"I know," Luther said.

Ruby passed the picture to Mom. "Can you believe Luther took that?"

Chip peered over Mom's shoulder and saw why they were so impressed. It was a perfect picture of two little panthers, one front-on to the camera, the other sideways as it leapt through the air to pounce on the first one.

Mom peered closely at the picture, and said, "These kittens are spotted, like—I don't know—like an ocelot or something. Aren't Florida panthers tan?"

"The adults are," Chip said. "But the babies are spotted, so their mothers can hide them."

"Where *is* the mother?" Mom asked.

"Yeah," Ruby echoed in alarm. "Where's the mother?"

Lily said, "We figure they're orphans."

"Those fat little fellas aren't orphans," Mr. Wilson said. "Their mama's right there."

"Where?" everybody in the room seemed to ask at once.

"In this picture." Mr. Wilson handed his snapshot to the Hashimotos. "And probably in that one you're holding, Mrs. Martin."

Mom stared hard at her picture. "I don't see—"

"Look again, Betty," Booker said. "Don't you see two red dots in amongst the trees behind the kittens?"

"I see something that looks like the lit ends of cigarettes," Ruby said.

"Those are no lit cigarettes," Mr. Wilson told her. "Those are the eyes of a mama panther, keeping close watch on her babies."

"Really?" Luther grabbed one of the pictures and stared at it for a moment. "I did it!" he yelled. "I actually got a picture of a grown panther in the wild!"

"Oh my gosh!" Chip breathed.

"Heaven help us!" Mrs. Hashimoto looked liked she was going to faint. "Lily, I can't believe you were out in the woods with a panther prowling about! You could have been killed!"

"And *eaten*," Lily added.

He elbowed Lily in the ribs. "Worse than that. She could've eaten your soccer ball."

Luther, Chip, and Lily giggled, but Mrs. Wilson put a stop to that in a hurry. "This is serious, children. Tell them, Sam. You remember when this area was much wilder than it is now, back when farmers had problems with panthers stealing the livestock."

Mr. Wilson nodded. "Mostly it was a problem for farmers closer to the swamp, but once a panther snatched one of our kid goats. My daddy and me tracked it down to the big canal and found where the panther had laid up to eat that kid."

"What did you do?" Luther asked, his eyes wide.

"Nothing we could do," his grandfather replied. "The panther was long gone by the time we got there. Wasn't nothing left of the little kid goat but four hooves and a patch of hide."

"Panthers *eat* goats?" Chip asked in dismay.

Mr. Wilson glanced at Chip. "Why wouldn't they? Goats aren't all that different from deer, which is what they eat in the wild."

"Wonder what they find to eat on the Old Place?" Booker mused. "It's only ten acres."

"Oh no," Luther moaned. "So that's what happened to the rabbits."

"You're right," Chip said, feeling queasy. "There used to be lots of them. A couple of months ago we counted sixty-seven."

"And now?" Booker asked. "How many?"

"Not that many," Chip mumbled.

"How many?" Booker asked again. "Last count?"

"Fourteen," Lily said.

In the quiet tone Booker always used when he wanted you to think seriously about something, he asked, "So what do you kids figure that mama panther's going to feed her cubs when she runs out of rabbits?"

Chip stared at his feet. He loved the rabbits. But he also loved the panther kittens. Why did it have to be one or the other?

Mr. Wilson said, "One thing's for absolute certain. We are not having any panthers filling their bellies with our goats. Nor with our children either."

"Who should we call to deal with this?" Mr. Hashimoto asked. "We need someone who can get those animals out of there *now*."

"They're an endangered species!" Luther cried. "They should be left alone!"

"I only told you because I wanted you to understand why we have to keep builders away from the Old Place!" Chip said, desperately wishing he'd kept his mouth shut. "The panthers *live* there! Can't they stay?"

"The answer to that," Mom said, "is an absolute and final no. Those animals have to go, and until they're gone"—she looked around at the other parents—"I assume none of us want our children to leave their own yards, except to go to the bus stop."

"See?" Luther said angrily to Chip. "I told you they're going to keep us under house arrest until we're grown."

"Well, now," Mr. Wilson said thoughtfully. "I doubt it'll be quite that long." He looked over at Mr. Hashimoto. "If you don't mind me taking off work this weekend, I think I know somebody who can deal with those cats."

"Yes, certainly," Mr. Hashimoto said with relief. "Take as much time as you need." He and his wife stood up to leave. "It'll be a relief to have all this settled."

Chip dared to squeak out one more question: "What about the Old Place?"

But the other adults were already getting to their feet and didn't hear him. So many of them standing so close made Chip feel small and hopeless. He'd let the secret out about the panther kittens, and all for nothing. Not only was he going to lose the Old Place, he was going to lose the panthers too.

Justin, though, had apparently heard Chip's question. He frowned and said something to Booker, who rolled his wheelchair out in front. The others waited, to let him go through the door first, but he used the wheelchair to block the door. With a big grin he asked, "Am I understanding right, that everybody in this room is going to do everything they can to keep Blake from going ahead?"

"Definitely!" said Mr. Hashimoto. "I intend to call every single county commissioner this weekend and make it clear that we do not want a meatpacking plant out this way. If they persist, *we* will get a lawyer."

"You might want to call the members of the variance committee too," Kate said. "I've got a list with all their names and phone numbers."

"Give it to me," Mom said. "I'll make copies and we'll all call."

"I'll call," Ruby promised, "and keep calling. Nobody should be able to come into our neighborhood and throw up any old thing. You don't see them putting meatpacking plants in rich folks' neighborhoods!"

Ruby collected Luther's pictures and handed them back to him. "Luther," she said, "I'm real proud of you, and I'm sorry I got on your case about that protest. If it wasn't for you and your friends, Blake would be running roughshod over the law and all of us by now." Ruby looked at Mom. "What do you say, Betty? Do we have some outstanding kids here or what?"

Mom's face, which had looked worried and angry for two days, relaxed into a happy smile. "Absolutely, Ruby. They aren't always the best-behaved kids, but they might be the smartest." Still smiling, she added, "Including you, Brad."

When everybody had driven away, Mom, Kate, and Justin went back into the house. Chip stayed outside by himself for a good long while, looking up at the star-filled sky. Everything had turned out the way he wanted it to—except for one thing.

In trying to save the Old Place, he had given away the panthers' secret.

25

A Dangerous Day

On Saturday morning Chip got up early to do his chores. After feeding the ducks, he walked down to Lost Goat Lane and turned toward the Old Place.

First he went to the front of the property where the old cow pen used to be. There was no grass there anymore because Blake's bulldozer had plowed it up. But a little farther back, near the bramble patch, Chip figured he might be able to see the rabbits one more time. He was just putting out some grain when he heard his name drifting down from the sky. "Hey, Chip! About time you got here."

Actually, the voice didn't come from the sky. It came from the loft of the old barn. Chip looked up and saw Lily's face peering out.

"Thought you were under house arrest," he called up to her.

"Thought you were." Her face disappeared from the hole, and in a minute she was on the ground next to him.

"How'd you know I'd be here?" he asked.

"You had to come," she said simply. "To say goodbye to the kittens. Just like I had to say goodbye to Miguel and the others."

She was right. Chip had turned the idea of coming to say goodbye over and over in his mind the night before, thinking how dangerous it could be if the mother panther decided it was *not* okay for him to be there and came after him. He counted the rabbits that had come out to nibble at the grain. There were eight left, so he knew the panthers hadn't run out of food. If the mother panther decided to attack, it would be because she was scared or mad, not because she was hungry. He thought again about how dangerous it would be to go into the Jungle—how dangerous it had been all along.

But he just *had* to see those kittens one last time. "You shouldn't come with me," he told Lily. "It could be dangerous."

"Get real!" she said. "You think I'm going to let you go back there alone? I want to say goodbye to them too. Besides, if that mother panther eats you, somebody has to tell your mom. Otherwise nobody would know what became of you."

Chip didn't waste any more breath trying to convince her to stay behind. He'd learned a long time ago that it was practically impossible to keep Lily from doing something she wanted to do. He followed her across the torn-up earth back to the road.

They weren't surprised when they saw Luther tearing down the road toward them. They stopped at the end of the trail through the cornfield and waited for him.

"Thanks...for waiting," Luther panted as he slid to a stop next to them.

They jogged along between the rows of corn and jumped the ditch. Then, making as little noise as possible, they slipped through the bushes. Once they reached the more open part of the woods, they spread out a little—Chip in the middle, with Luther and Lily about three feet away on either side. They stopped often to look and listen. All they could hear were the usual sounds of chirping birds and occasionally a small animal scurrying in the underbrush.

It was dim in the forest, but up ahead Chip could see a

bright spot where sunshine was spilling down onto the pond. Suddenly there were no more trees in front of him and his eyes focused on the knoll. His feet stopped moving, and for a minute he could barely breathe. All he managed to do was stretch out an arm on either side and wiggle his fingers for Luther and Lily to stop. They froze.

A long tan panther lay stretched out on the highest part of the grassy knoll. Her head was lifted and her bright golden eyes stared straight at them. Chip felt hypnotized, like he couldn't look away from her gaze if he wanted to. She was so incredibly beautiful, he just wanted to look and look and memorize every tiny detail about her.

But beautiful as she was, she wasn't the star. The kittens, who seemed twice as big as they'd been less than a week earlier, were scrapping over something bloody on the ground beside her. As they romped and played tug-of-war with the carcass, Chip got a glimpse of a long ear, the kind of ear you don't see on armadillos or raccoons or possums. But he pushed that to the back of his mind. There were too many other fascinating details in the scene that he wanted to take in and never forget for as long as he lived.

The kittens seemed unaware of them, but the mother panther was fully alert. She continued to stare straight into Chip's eyes. With every muscle in her body tensed, she was ready to spring up and defend her kittens.

We won't hurt them, he told her in his mind. *We just came to say goodbye.*

Chip took a small step backward, then another and another. On either side of him Luther and Lily were doing the same. In a few steps, trees came between them and the panthers so Chip couldn't see them anymore. But he kept backing up. He was afraid that if he and Lily and Luther turned and ran, the mother panther might mistake them for food.

They didn't run, and the panther didn't come after them. She must have decided that they weren't food after all.

Or maybe she just wasn't hungry.

When they reached Lost Goat Lane, they stopped. "My mom went to the doctor this morning," Lily said. "If she's back already, she'll probably punish me by burning all my soccer shorts. But if I can get home before she does, she'll never know."

"I don't think I'll get caught either," Chip said. "Unless Kate or Justin tells Mom. But I'm pretty sure they won't."

Luther didn't say anything. He just stood there looking toward the Wilson place with his face pinched up.

"What about you, Luther?" Chip asked. "How'd you get out, anyway, with so many grown-ups around?"

"Uncle Booker took Mama and Grandma to town a little while ago," Luther said. "Then a man came to see Grandpa. I disappeared while they were talking."

"Somebody wanting to bring Old Billy another wife?" Chip asked.

Luther shook his head. "I'd never seen this person before. He wasn't black, but he had dark skin and straight black hair." Luther hesitated, then added, "I think he might be a Native American."

"What makes you think that?" Lily asked.

"You know how at the meeting Grandpa said he might know someone who could deal with the panthers? Well, I heard Grandpa tell Mama last night that the person he had in mind is his friend from the Big Cypress Reservation."

"How's he going to deal with them?" Chip asked, with a prickle of alarm.

Luther wrapped his arms around himself, looking miserable.

"The man came in a pickup truck." Luther's voice dropped almost to a whisper. "There's a gun rack in the back. With a gun in it."

The three of them stood in silence for at least one whole minute. Then, without saying a word, they started running toward the Wilson place.

When they got close to the house, they slowed down to a walk. The first thing they saw was a white pickup truck with an extended cab, plus a camper shell on the back. They also saw the rifle in the gun rack behind the backseat.

Mr. Wilson and the stranger were sitting on the front porch drinking coffee. The man's straight black hair was pulled into a ponytail that reached to the collar of his white T-shirt. He was looking at Luther's pictures. Mr. Wilson was studying a map of Florida. They laid the map and pictures aside as Luther, Chip, and Lily came up on the porch.

"Luther," Mr. Wilson said. "Did I just see you walking up that road?"

"Yes, Grandpa," Luther said.

"Didn't your mama tell you not to leave the house?"

"Yes, Grandpa."

"What about you other children?" Mr. Wilson asked. "I know I heard your parents tell you to stay home till these panthers are dealt with."

"Yes sir," Chip and Lily replied together.

"So how is it that you come to be walking up the road from the direction of the Old Place?"

Instead of answering Mr. Wilson's question, Lily looked at the other man and asked, "Are you a Native American?"

"Yes, I am," he said, his voice rumbling deep down in his chest. "I am a Seminole Miccosukee."

"Mick-oh-soo-kee," Lily repeated slowly, getting the pronunciation almost right.

"What's going to happen to our panthers?" Chip asked.

"*Your* panthers?" The man said it like he thought that was the weirdest thing he ever heard. "Panthers don't belong to people. They belong to themselves."

"But are you going to...you know...hurt them?" Chip asked. Even though he was going on thirteen, he felt tears coming to his eyes.

"Please don't," Luther said, almost choking on the words.

Mr. Wilson sighed. "So that's what this sudden rebellion is all about. Well, I reckon you kids are going to be in for it when your mamas get home. But in the meantime, you might as well sit down here with Jumper and me and hear what he's intending to do."

Chip, Lily, and Luther sat down together on the porch swing. Chip was no longer worried about what Mom might do when she found out he had disobeyed her. He didn't care. All he cared about was the panther family.

"Jumper's an old friend of mine, from when we were in the army together," Mr. Wilson explained. "We didn't stay in touch much after we got out, but I saw his name in the paper a few years back, about how he was helping reintroduce a panther down in the Glades."

"Reintroduce?" Chip asked.

"It means taking an animal that somehow got displaced from its natural habitat back to where it belongs," Jumper explained. He reached for the map and folded it open. "This area down here," he said, and waited for Chip, Luther, and Lily to crowd around to see where his finger was pointing. "This is the Florida Panther Reserve. We can't be sure this particular panther came from there, but it's a good guess. She had to have been pregnant, because she sure didn't take off through farming country with kittens trailing after her. I'd be willing to bet she came from there, or somewhere close by. If we can get her back to that general area, she'll find her own way to whatever part of the Everglades she considers home."

"Jumper's willing to take the cats out of here if he can catch them," Mr. Wilson said.

Luther looked doubtful. "You might catch the kittens, but I don't know about the mama."

A faint smile appeared on Jumper's face. "Oh, I've downed a few grown panthers in my time."

"What does that mean, downed?" Lily practically shrieked.

"You don't shoot them, do you?" Chip asked nervously.

"In a manner of speaking, yes." Without bothering to explain what he meant, he got up and walked out to his truck. When he came back, he was carrying a gun, but not the one from the gun rack. To Chip it looked more like an air rifle.

Jumper held it so they could see it. "Dart gun," he said. "It shoots a hypodermic needle into the cat's hide. The hypo is filled with a tranquilizer. That puts her out." He paused, then added, "Can't use it on kittens, though. Wildcats are supersensitive to drugs. You tranquilize a kitten and it might not wake up."

"You wouldn't take the mother without the kittens, would you?" Luther asked.

"No, I'll trap the little ones," Jumper said. "After the mama's out cold, of course."

Terms like *puts her out* and *out cold* frightened Chip. "Are you sure it won't hurt her?" he asked.

Jumper looked steadily at Chip. His coal black eyes didn't promise anything, and neither did his words. "When humans go messing with wild animals, you never know what's going to happen. Sometimes even a grown cat has a bad reaction to the tranquilizer. Or maybe she wakes up too soon and hurts herself trying to escape."

"What if she dies?" Luther asked. "What would happen to the kittens?"

"I'd take them someplace where they could be looked after by professionals who know what they're doing. Otherwise they'd starve to death." He looked at Mr. Wilson. "Normally a job like this can take days, even weeks. But the area they're in is so small—around ten acres, you said? And no one on nearby farms has lost any animals?"

"That's right," Mr. Wilson said.

"Then I should be able to find where they're laying up right off."

"We'll come and show you," Luther offered.

"No," Jumper said. "This is a one-man job."

"More like a two-man job," Mr. Wilson said. "Once the mama's in that big cage you brought, it's going to be more than you can carry by yourself."

"I can manage," Jumper said.

"Yeah?" Mr. Wilson grinned. "Cause while I'm an old man, you're still the same twenty-five-year-old you were back when we were in the army together? No way, Jumper. When you head into that swamp, it's going to be *two* old men, both pretending we're still as strong as we ever were."

"Couldn't we just wait in the truck?" Chip pleaded.

Mr. Wilson looked at Jumper, who gave a small shrug which wasn't yes, but wasn't no.

"Well, first off," Mr. Wilson said, "this is something Jumper and me need to discuss in private, because when I asked him to come do us this favor, there wasn't any mention of him babysitting a bunch of kids who don't mind any too well."

"We'll mind you!" Lily cried. "We'll do *anything* you tell us."

"Second thing," Mr. Wilson said. "Nobody's coming unless

their mama says it's okay. And I got a feeling your mamas, when they find out where you went this morning, are not going to be too agreeable."

"Can we ask anyway?" Lily persisted.

"You can ask," Mr. Wilson said. "But even if *they* say yes, that don't mean Jumper and me are saying yes. Some jobs are just way easier without an audience."

Then Luther spoke up. "I want to work in wildlife conservation when I grow up, Jumper. I'm already a good observer, and a pretty good photographer. But I don't have much experience with actual animals. It would help me a lot to see what you do."

Chip thought this was a brilliant move on Luther's part.

Jumper looked at Luther a good long time. Finally he said, "That'll be for your parents to decide." Then Jumper cut his black eyes over at Mr. Wilson and said, "You know, Sam, I was out tracking and trapping with my dad when I was a lot younger than these kids. Bet you were too."

26
Waiting

Chip and Lily left Luther's at a gallop, headed for the Hashimoto nursery to talk to their parents. But as soon as Chip saw all the cars in the parking lot, he knew this wasn't a good time. Mom wasn't going to let him interrupt her with a question when there was a line of people waiting to check out—not unless it was a matter of life and death. Which Chip felt like it was, but she probably wouldn't see it that way.

"Oh no!" Lily groaned when she saw her dad surrounded by customers. "I'll have to ask my *mother.*"

Chip decided to go home and watch from the porch until the parking lot emptied out, then run across and talk to Mom. But just as he reached the porch he met Justin coming out of the house.

"Justin!" Chip exclaimed. "Where're you going?"

"Over to the nursery to see Mom," Justin said.

"Wait—you gotta help me! You won't believe what's going on." Barely stopping for breath, he told Justin about Jumper and how he was going to capture the panthers and take them to the Everglades, and how he would let Chip watch only if his mother gave permission, and would Justin *please* ask her because Chip knew that no matter how busy Mom was, she'd take time to talk to Justin and listen to whatever he had to say.

Justin's expression grew more and more incredulous as Chip went on. "Wow!" he exclaimed when Chip finally stopped for breath. "Now *there's* something *I'd* like to see! But I think Booker wants to drive back to Atlanta this afternoon."

"Will you ask her if I can go with Jumper?" Chip pleaded.

"Sure." Justin gave Chip's shoulder a brotherly punch and headed off down the driveway. Chip stood on the porch and watched him as he walked across the highway and toward the shelter in the middle of the nursery where Mom worked the cash register. Then the phone rang inside the house.

It was Luther, calling to say Ruby had just come home. "She said yes!" he shouted into the phone. "But not to the Jungle," he added. "I'll have to wait in the truck at the Old Place."

"When are you leaving?" Chip asked.

"Pretty soon," Luther replied.

"I'll call you back," Chip said and slammed down the phone. He was halfway out to the porch when the phone rang again. It was Lily, howling mad, saying that both her mother and her father had absolutely forbidden her to go.

"That's too bad," Chip said. He listened to her story for a minute until she had to go, then he hung up feeling really sorry for her.

But he had problems of his own. What if Mom heard Mr. Hashimoto say no? Would his refusal influence her to say no too? Then Chip had an idea. He called the Wilsons' house and asked Ruby if *she* would call Mom and explain why she thought it was a good idea for him and Luther to go along.

"Listen, Chip," Ruby said, "I think this whole thing is a terrible idea. But the rest of the family ganged up on me to let Luther go. Even Richard thinks it would be educational."

"But...but you don't want Luther going by himself, do you, Ruby? Wouldn't it be better if I waited in the truck with him?"

"I don't know about that either," Ruby retorted. "Sometimes I think when you two get together, you're more trouble than *four* ordinary boys."

Chip could tell she was teasing, so he laughed. "No, Ruby! We're good kids. You said so yourself last night."

"Did I say that? I must've been talking about some other kids." Then Ruby stopped teasing Chip and said, "Okay, I'll call your mom."

"Thanks!" Chip hung up and went back out to the porch. The parking lot was less crowded now. He closed his eyes and pictured Justin talking to Mom in his serious, nearly grown-up way. "Please, Mom," Chip whispered, crossing his fingers. "Say yes!"

The phone rang, and he ran to answer it. It was Luther again. "Hey, Chip! Guess what? After Mr. Jumper catches the panthers, I get to go with him to the Everglades to release them!"

"When?" Chip demanded. He was so jealous he could hardly stand it.

"As soon as he catches them. He'll have to leave right away so he can get there before the tranquilizer wears off. Can you go?"

"I can't find out because you're on the phone!" Chip snapped. "Wait!" he shouted. "Don't hang up. Let me talk to your grandpa."

Luther called Mr. Wilson to the phone.

"Mr. Wilson," Chip said. "Please, will you call my mom and ask her if I can come along with you and Mr. Jumper and Luther? You know, so she understands we'll be safe in the truck and all that?"

"I reckon I could do that," Mr. Wilson said. "Booker's just heading down that way. He can tell her too."

It felt like five hours, but really it was only about five minutes before Chip saw Booker's van pull up in front of the nursery and then Mom and Justin walking out to the van to talk to Booker. Chip was wondering whether he should go over and start begging when they looked toward the house. Seeing Chip on the porch, Mom smiled and waved. And Justin gave him a thumbs-up.

Chip rushed into the house and called Luther. "I'm coming!" he said breathlessly. "Don't let them leave without me!"

He ran all the way. By the time he got to the Wilsons', the others were in the truck. They drove straight to the Old Place and parked by the trail through the cornfield.

"You boys get back there in the camper shell and scoot the traps out to Sam and me," Jumper said.

The traps looked like large pet carriers, but with special doors designed to snap shut when an animal entered. As Chip slid one toward the back door, it squawked. He jumped so hard he bumped his head on the camper shell. "What's in there?" he yelped.

"Bait," said Jumper.

Luther peered in. "It's a *chicken.*"

"A *live* chicken?" Chip asked, rubbing the top of his head.

"Did you ever hear a dead one squawk?" Luther asked.

"What're you going to do with it?" Chip asked Jumper.

"Tie it out in an open area to attract the mother panther. I'll be hiding close by, waiting to get a dart into her," Jumper explained.

"That'll be pretty scary for the chicken," Chip muttered.

Jumper gave him a look. "That chicken isn't going to suffer as much as those supermarket chickens that are raised in small cages. This chicken's had a good free-ranging life up to now. It won't like being staked out, but I can tell you, when that cat pounces, it'll happen so fast the chicken won't even have time to be scared."

"Oh," Chip said.

"Now," said Jumper. "How do we get into this area where the panthers are?"

"You have to walk along the corn rows." Chip pointed toward the ditch. "There's a place toward the back where it's easy to cross. Once you're on the other side, you go through some bushes until they thin out and the trees get big. A little way past that there's an open area by a swampy pond. That's where we always see them."

Jumper listened carefully, then said, "Okay. Sam, how about we carry this big cage and let the boys bring the traps?"

Chip and Luther exchanged excited glances. They were going to get to watch the trapping after all!

Jumper handed Mr. Wilson the dart gun. Then he reached for the rifle.

Chip stared. "What do you need the gun for?"

"I spent my life trying to protect panthers," Jumper said, "and I hope I never have to kill one. But a full-grown panther can kill a man. If it comes down to her or me, it ain't gonna be me."

He picked up one end of the big cage, and Mr. Wilson picked up the other end. Lugging it between them, they walked through the cornfield. Luther followed carrying one trap and Chip followed with the other, the chicken inside clucking nervously all the way. By the time they got to the place where they always jumped the ditch, Chip felt like his arms were going to fall off.

Jumper and Mr. Wilson waded right into the ditch with the big cage, even though the water was up to their hips. The big cage was empty, but it was heavy. And Chip knew that when they brought it back across with a panther in it, it was going to be a lot heavier. Mr. Wilson was strong for an old man, and Jumper's muscles bulged under his white T-shirt. Still, Chip couldn't see how they'd be able to handle it by themselves.

Jumper and Mr. Wilson waded back for the traps, carried them across the ditch, then returned one more time for the dart gun and the rifle. "Now you boys go back to the truck," Jumper said.

"Can't we come along and watch?" Chip begged. "We'll stay out of the way."

Jumper shook his head. "Tranquilizing an animal is not a pretty sight."

"Go back," Mr. Wilson said, pointing the way they'd come. "And I mean *all* the way back. If you plan to go to the Glades with us, you wait at the truck. You understand?"

Chip and Luther trudged out to the road and settled down to wait. One hour passed, then another. It was so hot in the truck that they got out and sat next to it, even though it was just about high noon and there was very little shade. But they didn't venture anywhere near the cornfield or the ditch. They didn't even go to the old barn to count rabbits. They just waited.

They both jumped up when they heard a shot that sounded like an air rifle. "The dart gun!" Chip said excitedly, thinking that now they wouldn't have to wait much longer. A few minutes later they heard another gunshot, this time a real one.

Chip jumped up and started for the cornfield, but Luther caught his arm. "No! We have to stay here." So they sat down again in the thin strip of shade next to the truck, their backs against one of its big tires. Chip glanced over at Luther. He sat with his legs drawn up and his head on his knees. Even though Luther's face was turned away from him, Chip knew he was worrying about what that second shot meant.

At last they heard someone coming. Mr. Wilson emerged from the cornfield and said, "Okay, boys. Now we need your help."

When they got to the ditch, Mr. Wilson said, "Go ahead, cross over. You said you wanted to see how this kind of thing is done. Well, now you're going to see. Like Jumper said, it's not a pretty sight."

Chip thought about the mother panther lying on the grassy knoll in the sunshine, her tan head lifted high, ears tilted toward him, those golden eyes staring straight into his. That was the way he wanted to remember her. If something bad had happened to her, he didn't want to see it.

He hesitated on the rim of the ditch. Then he jumped.

27
Panthers Up Close

The mother panther wasn't in the exact same spot where Chip had seen her before, but nearby, in the cage. She was lying very still. There was blood on the ground.

Jumper squatted on his haunches and peered through the slats. "Healthier than I expected. Usually when they stray into a farming area, they just about starve to death. Or else take after somebody's livestock and get shot. This one looks like she's been living on the fat of the land."

"The fat of our rabbits," Luther murmured.

"*Your* rabbits?" Jumper grinned up at him. "I bet she thinks they were put here for her."

"Is she…dead?" Chip asked.

Jumper looked at him in surprise. "Course not. Can't you see her breathing?"

Chip hadn't looked closely because he was afraid that if he did, he'd see a bullet hole in her sleek tan hide. He squatted next to Jumper and peered through the slats. Her sides were moving up and down very gently. Her mouth was open, drooling. It almost made him sick to see her like that, but at least she wasn't dead.

"We heard a shot," Luther said.

Jumper waved a black fly away from his face. "I was signaling to Sam that I'd darted her. I wanted some help dragging her into the cage."

"Where did the blood come from?" Chip asked, motioning to the blood-spattered grass.

"The chicken," Jumper said. "Nothing attracts a wildcat like a bird on the ground. She saw that chicken and *whap!* Killed it faster than you can blink an eye. Then she started pulling its feathers off, getting ready to eat it. That's when I darted her."

"What about the kittens?" Luther interrupted.

"She had them stashed in the trees, so they could see how a panther is supposed to make a kill. Soon as she passed out, I cut the chicken in half and put some in each trap. The cubs were nervous at first, upset because their mama wasn't responding to them, but hungry too. They couldn't resist that fresh meat." He paused. "There was just one slipup."

"What?" Chip asked.

"They both went into one trap and started fighting over the same piece of chicken. So they got trapped together."

"Where are they?" Chip asked.

Jumper pointed into the woods. "Over there in the shade. First we'll get the mama out of here, then come back for them."

"Can we see them?" Luther asked.

"Later. This tranquilizer will only last about three hours—meaning we got no time to waste. I don't want to have to dart her again."

Jumper and Mr. Wilson each grabbed handles at the front of the cage, leaving Chip and Luther to take the handles at the back. Chip could see that it was made especially for holding dangerous animals. There was no place she could get her face or paws through to bite or claw them, even if she had been awake.

By the time they got to the truck, Chip was wet from sneakers to waist from wading across the ditch, and his T-shirt was drenched in sweat. As soon as the cage was loaded into the back of the truck, Jumper turned around and almost ran back down the trail. The others followed at a trot, breathing hard.

Chip thought it would be easier carrying the kittens, but he was wrong. Even though they didn't weigh as much as the mother, they were scared and kept throwing their weight from side to side, which made it harder to balance the trap between the four of them. One minute there would be hardly any weight in Chip's corner, and the next minute it would feel like he was carrying the whole thing by himself. Jumper rushed them so fast that Chip hardly got a chance to see the kittens. It wasn't until they slid the trap into the truck that he got a good look at them. When the kittens saw him peering in, they reared back on their haunches, growling like they were the biggest, meanest tigers in the world. But Chip could see in their eyes how scared they were, and it almost broke his heart.

"Can we ride back here with them?" Chip asked.

"No," Jumper said. "In the cab. But first help me tie down the cages."

He climbed into the back of the pickup and began lashing down the cages so they wouldn't slide around. Chip and Luther were handing him another length of rope when a car pulled up.

It was the Hashimotos' big Buick. Mr. Wilson walked over to speak to Lily's parents. A minute later she leapt out of the car and ran to the back of the truck. "You caught them!"

Mr. and Mrs. Hashimoto followed their daughter and peered into the truck bed at the captured panthers. The kittens had stopped snarling and were crouched in the back corner of their cage, looking small and frightened.

"The little ones are darling," remarked Mrs. Hashimoto. "They don't look very dangerous."

"I don't see how they could possibly get out of those cages," Mr. Hashimoto said. "And the mother is completely sedated. It looks safe enough."

The Hashimotos and Mr. Wilson huddled for a few minutes, talking in low voices. Jumper climbed out of the truck and joined them. Then the Hashimotos got into their Buick and drove away without Lily.

"Well, Jumper," Chip heard Mr. Wilson say as the men returned to the pickup. "Looks like you got one more junior biologist in your wildlife rescue class."

Jumper grinned. "No problem, as long as it's only three. If we collect any more, though, we might have to put the kids in the cages and let the panthers have the backseat."

By the time Jumper and Mr. Wilson had their seat belts fastened, Chip, Luther, and Lily were all buckled up in the backseat.

"I thought you weren't allowed," Chip said to Lily.

Lily shrugged. "It was a negotiation."

"What do you mean?" asked Luther.

"Don't you know what negotiating is?" Lily asked.

"Sure," Luther said. "But how do you always manage to get what you want?"

"You have to know what your *parents* want," Lily said. "In my case that's easy, because they tell me over and over. You just give them something they want in exchange for what you want."

The pickup bounced along Lost Goat Lane. When they reached the main highway, Jumper sped up. Soon they were flying along a straight highway through flat countryside, with sugarcane fields on both sides. Then the cane fields vanished, and for a while they drove through an area with dead trees on both sides of the highway.

"What happened to all the trees?" Luther asked.

"It's all these canals and new housing developments. That's changed the way water flows into the Glades," Jumper said over his shoulder. "Trees don't much like change. When water stands too long around them, they die. And when they don't get as much water as they're used to, they die."

Chip looked out at the forest of dead trees. "Where we're taking the panthers, are there live trees there?"

"Oh yeah," said Jumper. "And plenty of wildlife." He glanced at them in the rearview mirror. "That's going to be your job, protecting these last wild places. That's why I decided to bring you kids along. I want you to see some real panther habitat. If you don't work to save it, it's going to disappear and these cats will die with it. Can't anything survive once its habitat is destroyed."

"When will we get there?" Lily asked.

"Before nightfall, I hope. I don't fancy running my boat through the marsh in the dark."

"We're going in a *boat?*" Luther asked excitedly.

"Airboat," Jumper said. "That's the only way to get back in where it'll be safe to release them."

Luther started telling Lily about a boat he rode in once when he lived up north. Chip had heard the story before, so he stopped listening and just watched the dead trees whip by. Then he heard Jumper say to Mr. Wilson in a low voice, "You realize we're working under the radar."

"How's that?" Mr. Wilson asked.

"To do a proper release, you hold a cat in captivity for a

month or so and run a lot of tests to make sure it's healthy before setting it back in the wild. I've done plenty of those, and that's a good way to do it. But I got my own ideas too."

"Such as?" Mr. Wilson asked.

"This cat probably came out of the Glades no more than a month ago. She looks as fit as a fiddle, and she's got wild-born young. Take her and those kittens and stick them in a cage for a month, and it'll make it that much harder for them to readapt. I figure the quicker this family is back in its natural habitat, the better."

"You're the expert," Mr. Wilson said. "All I want is to get them moved to where they don't pose a danger to us. I'm much obliged to you for making that happen."

"Hey," Jumper said. "You saved my life in Nam. The least I could do was keep panthers from gobbling up your old goats." He seemed to notice that Luther had stopped talking and that he and Chip and Lily were listening. "Although," he added for their benefit, "there's a good chance she'd have gone after these kids first."

"No, she wouldn't!" Chip protested. "Her kittens were already getting to be our friends. The mother knew we wouldn't hurt them."

"What she knew," said Jumper, "was that you didn't look like anything she'd eaten before. She was watching you, making up her mind. That's how all the big cats do. If it's an animal they've eaten before, and they happen to be hungry, they take it. But if it's something unfamiliar, they watch awhile."

"You think she would have...?" Luther began, letting his voice trail off.

"I *know* she would have," Jumper said quietly. "It was just a question of time. You kids are lucky to be alive."

They rode in silence for a long time after that.

28

The Glades

They were deep in the Everglades when Jumper pulled into the driveway of a small house with a large screened-in porch. Behind the house, a wooden dock stuck out into a reed-filled waterway. Tied up at the dock was a flat-bottomed boat with a square nose instead of a pointy one. At the back of the boat was something like an airplane propeller inside a cage. Chip figured the cage was to keep people from accidentally getting cut by the propeller when it was turning.

A stout woman with dark skin and curly black hair opened the door of the house and called, "There you are, Jumper! I was beginning to wonder if you were going to make it back in time for supper." When she saw the kids getting out of the pickup she said, "You should've let me know you were bringing visitors."

Chip noticed good cooking smells coming from the house. He had skipped lunch and was glad supper was almost ready.

"I'm not back," Jumper called to her. "Not for a couple of hours yet. Got a cat family to take home." He untied the trap with the kittens. "You boys carry this over to that dock," he said. Then he reached into the empty trap, brought out half a dead chicken, and handed it to Lily. "You better take this.

Those cubs might need more meat before their mama's awake enough to hunt."

Any other girl would have refused to touch the cut-in-half chicken with bloody entrails hanging out, Chip thought, or at least would have said "yuck!" Lily didn't say a word. She just took the dead chicken and followed Chip and Luther. Jumper and Mr. Wilson carried the big cage with the mother panther in it. When they reached the dock, Jumper got in the boat and had the others hand things in one at a time, so he could arrange them. "I forgot the guns," he said to Mr. Wilson. "Go back and get them, will you?"

As soon as Mr. Wilson came back with the guns, Jumper assigned everyone a place in the airboat. He sat in the back, in a seat that was higher than the others, to run the motor. Chip and Lily sat in the seat just ahead of Jumper, with Luther and Mr. Wilson in the front seat. The cages with the panthers were in the bow, leaving barely enough room for Mr. Wilson's and Luther's knees.

The engine roared, the propeller whirled, and they went zooming across the water. It wasn't like any river or pond or lake Chip had ever seen, and it certainly wasn't the ocean. The network of waterways looked barely two feet deep. *You'd have to have an airboat out here,* Chip thought. *Any other kind of motorboat would run aground in the shallow water.*

They skimmed along on the surface, the warm wind whipping their faces. They passed some places where the trees— mostly pine and cypress—were growing out of dry ground. In other places the trees grew in swampy areas, like parts of the Jungle at the Old Place. The waterway was lined with tall reeds, so it was often hard to see where water ended and land started. There were lots of birds and dozens of turtles.

Once, Luther pointed to his left. Chip saw a large alligator lying on the bank. They were close enough to see the fangs hanging over its bottom lip. Remembering the last time he and Luther had been that close to an alligator—when they were only seven years old—sent shivers down Chip's spine. He was glad that this time they were in a boat, going fast.

After they'd traveled nearly an hour, Chip lost interest in the scenery and started feeling how really hungry he was. He was relieved when Jumper turned toward shore and cut the engine. Using a long pole, he eased the boat through the reeds until its squarish prow was resting on something like solid ground.

"Wait here," Jumper said. He splashed into the shallow water, waded ashore, and disappeared into the trees.

Mr. Wilson reached into an old green canvas backpack with *US Army* printed on it and brought out a bottle of insect repellent. "You kids better rub on some of this," he advised. "They say the mosquitoes here in the Glades are so big it only takes four of them to carry off a grown man."

They laughed and smeared the smelly repellent on their bare skin. By the time everyone was thoroughly covered, Jumper was back. "Looks good," he said. "I didn't see any other panther marks around. Chances are, this family can get through the night without being bothered."

Chip could tell by the rocking of the boat that the mother panther was moving around a little. Jumper must have felt it too. "Not much time," he said. "Another few minutes and she'll be on her feet, armed and dangerous."

Mr. Wilson helped Jumper lift the big cage out of the boat. "You boys bring the cubs," Jumper said. "And don't forget that chicken," he added, nodding at Lily.

They splashed through the water and slogged across the soggy ground. When they reached a dry, grassy area at the edge of the woods, they set down the cage. Jumper motioned to Chip and Luther to put the kitten trap a few feet away, then took the half chicken from Lily and laid it on the ground between the two cages. "Okay," he called, "everybody back in the boat!"

"Can't we wait and see—" Lily started, but Jumper cut her off.

"In the boat," he said sharply, "now!"

Lily had the sense not to try to negotiate with Jumper. She ran back to the boat, followed by Luther. As Chip turned to run after them, he heard Jumper say to Mr. Wilson, "She won't be steady on her feet, but steady or not, she'll come out mad. And confused. There's not a reason in the world for her to head for the boat, but if she does, just make sure she never gets there."

"And if she goes for you?" Mr. Wilson asked.

Jumper grinned. "Didn't figure I had to tell you what to do if she goes for me."

Lily, Luther, and Chip climbed into the boat, but Mr. Wilson didn't. He took the rifle and moved a little closer to shore. Chip heard him click the safety off the gun. Mr. Wilson planned to shoot the mother panther if she went for Jumper or headed for the boat.

Chip, Luther, and Lily stood up on their seats so they could see over the reeds. The sun, low on the horizon, cast a path of golden light across the water. Sunshine hit the patch of grass where Jumper and the panthers were, and reflected off the metal fittings on the cages. Chip didn't know what he expected to happen, only what he was afraid *might* happen.

Standing to one side of the kitten trap, Jumper lifted the door. For a second nothing happened. Then the kittens came flying out like furry jacks-in-the-box. They bolted for the woods, then stopped. Chip thought later that it was like the mother had called to them, because they turned around, ran back, and sniffed at her cage.

Jumper had moved quickly to the mother cat's cage. The kittens backed off a little, snarling at him. Standing behind the big cage, Jumper reached over the top and jerked the door up. The mother cat came out like a shot and took a mighty leap.

Chip wasn't sure exactly what happened next, but it looked like she *stumbled*, like her front legs just collapsed under her. The mother panther went down on her side, hard. Before she could struggle to her feet, the kittens were on her, nuzzling to nurse. She tried to lift her head, and then, like she was just too tired, she dropped it onto the ground and lay there. A final ray of sunlight found its way through the tops of the reeds, giving the big cat's tan coat a golden hue. The last thing Chip saw was the rear ends of two hungry kittens as they nuzzled their mother's furry belly to get at that warm milk.

Then Jumper was there, yelling, "Sit down, kids!" He and Mr. Wilson swung the boat around to face the open water and the two old men piled in, whooping like teenagers. The engine roared and the boat went ripping through the reeds to the main channel.

Chip sat back, feeling like he had just watched the best movie of his life. He wanted to rewind and watch it all over again. He wanted to ask Jumper a million questions.

A part of him still wanted to hold those panther kittens and have them for pets. But he knew that would never happen, and should never happen. "They weren't ours," he whispered into the wind. "Panthers belong to themselves."

The sun set long before they got back to Jumper's place. It was the blackest dark night Chip had ever seen. At last they came around a bend in the waterway, and up ahead he saw a light at the end of a dock. Beyond it, rectangles of light shone through the windows of Jumper's house.

As they pulled in and scrambled up onto the dock, Chip saw thousands of moths and bugs buzzing around the bare lightbulb. He hadn't realized how many insects there were in the Everglades, and he was glad Mr. Wilson had remembered to bring repellent. Chip, Luther, and Lily stood on the dock with Mr. Wilson and waited. Jumper tied up the boat, then picked up the tranquilizer gun and the rifle and motioned for them to follow him to the house.

"What about the cages?" Chip asked. "Are you going back for them?"

"Oh, sure," Jumper said. "Tomorrow. The cats will be gone by then. Come daybreak, that mama will be on her feet, looking for fresh meat and a new home."

When they entered the kitchen, Chip saw that the table was already set with six places. Mrs. Jumper looked up from the fish she was frying. "Well, Jumper, you go into the Glades with three children, you come back with three. Looks like the *choo-wa-chobee* didn't get a one."

"*Choo-wa-chobee?*" Luther asked. "What's that?"

"That's what we Seminoles call a panther," Mrs. Jumper said as she forked up a huge platter of fried fish. "You never heard that?"

"No," Luther said. "Are you a Seminole too?"

"Sure am. Bet you didn't know there were Black Seminoles, did you? Some of my ancestors were runaway slaves. If I had time, I could tell you all kinds of stories about our people." Mrs. Jumper started dropping little balls of dough into the sizzling hot oil. "The bathroom's that way." She pointed a fork. "You all go wash up. Knowing Jumper and knowing children, there's no telling what you've got on your hands."

"Only dead chicken and smelly bug repellent," Lily said with a grin.

They washed up, then squeezed around a small table so filled with food that you could barely see the red tablecloth. Chip, his stomach rumbling with hunger, forked one whole fried fish onto his plate and added a pile of hush puppies and a heap of coleslaw. When he realized how much he had taken, he felt embarrassed and wondered if it would be worse manners to put some back.

Mrs. Jumper must have guessed what he was thinking. "I figured you'd all have a big appetite when you got here," she said. "There's plenty for everybody."

Lily speared a hush puppy on her fork. "Is this Seminole food?"

Everybody at the table laughed. "Child, don't you know what a hush puppy is?" Mr. Wilson said. "It's fried cornbread. That's not Seminole, that's Southern."

"I'm Southern," Lily said. "But my mother never makes hush puppies." She bit into the one on her fork. "But I wish she would. This tastes great."

Chip took a big swig of iced tea and asked, "What was that Seminole word for panther?"

"*Choo-wa-chobee*," Mrs. Jumper said, passing around the platter of hush puppies again. "In our language, that means 'big cat.'"

"The Florida panther is actually a kind of cougar," Jumper explained. "Other tribes have different names for it. The Cherokee name is *klandagi*, which means 'lord of the forest.' The Cree call it *katalgar*, which means 'greatest of wild hunters.'" He paused and looked over at his wife. "And don't the Chiksaws call it *ko-icto?*"

Mrs. Jumper nodded. "Yes. It means 'cat of God.'"

"Down in South America, the Quecha tribes call it *puma,*" Jumper added. "You may have heard that word. It means 'mighty magic animal.'"

"I *love* all those words!" Lily exclaimed. "I want to learn more about the Miccosukee-Seminole language." She stared at her empty plate. "And how to make hush puppies."

"Easiest thing in the world," Mrs. Jumper said. "Any girl who can eat as many as you ought to know how to make them. How about more iced tea, kids? Or Jumper, you and Sam want a cold beer?"

Mr. Wilson shook his head. "At my age, if I drink a glass of beer I fall asleep at the table. My wife won't put up with that!"

"None for me either," Jumper said. "I still got to drive these folks home."

"At this hour?" Mrs. Jumper cried. "Why don't you all stay the night?"

Chip and Luther exchanged glances. That was *exactly* what they'd been hoping for. If they were here in the morning, maybe they could go with Jumper to pick up the cages and see if the panthers were still around!

"We don't have enough beds, but we certainly got enough room," Mrs. Jumper said. "You kids wouldn't mind if I gave you each a blanket and pillow and let you curl up on the floor, would you?"

Jumper shook his head. "If it was just the boys, I'd say sure. But the little girl's parents were real nervous about her coming, and I promised I'd get her home tonight." Jumper pushed back his chair. "It's a good two-hour drive, so we'd better hit the road."

Lily scowled, but Chip noticed that she didn't argue with Jumper.

"I'll stay at Sam's place tonight," Jumper told his wife. "And head home in the morning after breakfast."

"I'm sorry to see you going to so much trouble on our account," Mr. Wilson said.

"What trouble? The kids will sleep on the drive back, and we'll have a couple more hours to talk about old times." Jumper grinned across the table at Chip, Luther, and Lily. "Sleeping kids are way less trouble than wide-awake ones." Then, to show he was just joking, he added, "Not that these three have been all that much trouble. They actually came in handy once or twice."

Chip carried his dishes to the sink just like he would at home, and the others did the same. He would have helped Mrs. Jumper wash them, but she had other ideas.

"Scat!" she said. "I don't tolerate kids in my kitchen, except for eating purposes. And Jumper is not a man to wait around. Better get yourselves out to that truck."

Luther, Lily, and Chip did fall asleep on the way home. Chip woke up when Lily climbed over him to get out at her house. It must have been long after midnight when Chip stumbled into bed. He was so sleepy he couldn't even keep his eyes open long enough to read the clock.

The last thing he thought before he fell asleep was that helping those panthers go free was probably the most important thing he'd ever done. And definitely the most exciting.

29
Double Whammy

When Chip heard Kate's voice it was morning and already a bright, hot day. "Are you going to sleep all day?" she asked.

That sounded like a good idea. Chip would have liked to lie there half-asleep for a while, remembering the day before.

"A really exciting thing happened while you were gone," Kate bubbled. "Oh, Chip, this is *so* wild, you won't *believe* it! Wait till I tell you!"

But then the phone rang and Kate ran to answer it. Chip gave up on the idea of going back to sleep and dragged himself out of bed. He felt more awake after he washed his face, awake enough to start wondering what Kate's news might be. On his way to the kitchen he saw that the living room floor was strewn with bride magazines and dress patterns and pieces of fabric—not denim like Kate and Ruby use to make their Denim Designs clothes, but flimsy, lacy kinds of material. He figured Kate's news probably had something to do with the wedding and wouldn't be as interesting to him as it was to her.

Kate hung up the phone and came into the kitchen.

"What time did Justin and Booker leave last night?" Chip asked.

"They didn't get off until early this morning," Kate said.

Chip was sorry he hadn't had a chance to tell Justin goodbye, but felt better when Kate added, "He said for you to send him an e-mail and let him know all about the panther release. He's dying to hear how it went."

While Kate talked, she poured him a glass of orange juice and put cereal and milk on the table, along with a bowl and spoon. Chip normally did this for himself. The fact that Kate set out breakfast for him meant she didn't just have something to say, it meant she wanted him to sit down and *listen.*

Chip reached for his glass, grumbling, "So what's so exciting about the wedding?"

"Not *wedding,* Chip. *Weddings!*" Kate practically screamed out the word *weddings.* Then she went bopping across the kitchen singing, "Here comes the bride."

Chip pitched his voice low and sang his own version: "Here comes the briiide. So fat and wiiide. See how she wobbles from side to siiiide."

Normally that would have bugged Kate, but she just laughed. "Oh, Chip, isn't it *awesome?* A double wedding!"

"Double wedding?" Chip repeated, pouring milk onto his cereal. "Ruby and Richard are going to get married *twice?*"

"No!" Kate stopped doing pirouettes and sat down at the table. "Mom's getting married too!"

The spoonful of cereal Chip was lifting fell out of his hand and plopped back into the bowl, sending a splatter of milk onto the table. "To Booker?"

"Of course! Who else is she on the phone with every night? Who else would have asked her?"

"I don't know," Chip said. "Did Booker ask her?"

"Nitwit! How could they be getting married if he didn't ask her?"

"Well, maybe *she* asked *him,*" Chip retorted, annoyed that

Kate had called him a nitwit for asking a perfectly reasonable question.

"She could have, I guess," Kate said. "But that doesn't matter. What matters is, they're getting married and it's going to be a *double wedding*. In the Wilsons' yard, with Mrs. Wilson's flowers all in bloom. It will be soooo beautiful!"

While Chip sat there trying to take it all in, Kate stopped chattering and gave him a worried look. "Mom was planning to tell us all together last night, but you went off and Justin was getting ready to leave, so, well, she told Justin and me last night and was going to tell you tonight. I guess I should've waited and let her…" Kate's voice trailed off.

"When?" Chip asked faintly.

"This summer. As soon as school's out and Booker gets back."

Chip picked up his unfinished cereal, carried it to the sink, and poured it down the garbage disposal. Booker might stay here for the summer, but what then? His stomach felt queasy. It was like being on a Tilt-A-Whirl, knowing you were going to be violently dumped one way or another, but not able to brace yourself because you didn't know which way you were going to go.

"How long will Booker be here? Stay here, I mean," Chip asked over his shoulder. What he really meant was, *How long will we go on living here? Will we be moving to Atlanta in the fall?*

"That," said Kate, "is the *really* big news. Only family knows."

Chip turned around. "What do you mean, *really* big news?"

"The high school baseball coach is retiring," Kate said.

"That's not news. Justin told me that last summer."

"The news," Kate said, "is that Booker applied for the job. Naturally he got it. What high school wouldn't want a college-level baseball coach? Especially one who used to be a star at that very same high school?"

Chip went out on the back porch and picked up the pail for milking the goats. Kate followed him. "I thought you'd be excited," she said. "Aren't you glad?"

"Sure," Chip said. "It's just that I didn't know."

"Nobody knew. Booker didn't even tell Mom until he knew for sure he'd be offered the job. He came by last night to tell her. If you'd been here you would've heard at the same time we did." Kate added a quick warning. "But we're going to keep it in the family till everything is official."

"What about Booker's family?" Chip asked.

"He probably told them last night too," Kate said.

Chip nodded and headed for the goat pen. He took as long as possible with the milking. Then he fed the ducks and stood watching them for a while. Normally the way they waddled around quacking like cartoon ducks made him smile. But not this morning. He couldn't forget how angry Luther was when Chip first told him about Mom and Booker kissing. And Luther still wasn't used to the idea of his mother marrying Mr. Jackson. When he found out that Booker and Mom were getting married, it would be a double whammy.

Chip felt he might be on the verge of a double whammy himself. The panther kittens had just vanished from his life. He was glad they were living free down in the Everglades, but he was going to be missing them for a long time. So he didn't know what he would do if, on top of that, he lost his best friend—again.

"Chip!" Kate called from the house. "It's hot out there. You better bring that milk in and get it in the fridge before it sours."

Chip plodded into the kitchen and strained the goat milk into jars. As he was putting it in the refrigerator, the phone rang.

"For you, Chip," Kate called. "It's Lily."

Chip didn't really feel like talking to Lily, but he went into the living room and took the phone from Kate. "Hello," he mumbled.

"Guess who I've been talking to!" Lily was shouting so loud that Chip probably could have heard her from across the street *without* a telephone.

"Somebody deaf?" Chip suggested. "Why are you yelling?"

"Who's yelling?" Lily barked. "Do you want to know or not?"

"Sure," Chip said. "Who have you been talking to?"

"Miguel!"

"He's back?" Chip asked.

"No. But he called yesterday while we were gone and left a number, so I called him this morning. He said the other community center kids got mobile homes to live in, everyone except him and his mom. They're not citizens, so they got stuck in a motel room until somebody figures out where to send them. He *hates* it."

"Is he going to have to go to school there?" Chip asked, thinking how hard it would be to go into a new school with only two weeks left in the term.

"Yes, and that's another thing. This will be his fourth school this year, with a lot of time missed in between. He's probably going to have to repeat seventh grade."

"Oh man, that stinks!" Chip said.

"Yeah, but just think, Chip. When I go into junior high next year, we'll be in the same grade!"

"What difference does that make if he's at a different school?" Chip asked.

"I'm working on that," Lily replied. "My mom's taking me to visit him and his mom this afternoon." Chip heard someone calling Lily's name. "Gotta go," she said. "See you later."

Chip hung up and stepped carefully through the wedding dress patterns and fabric samples scattered across the living room floor.

He went outside and wandered down Lost Goat Lane. He thought he was going to the Wilsons' to talk to Luther, but he veered off onto the dirt track and headed toward the Old Place instead. He knew he'd have to talk to his friend eventually, but he felt uncertain about—well, almost everything.

When he reached the Old Place, he sat down in the shade of the barn and tried to sort out his worries one at a time. Both Kate and Justin seemed okay with Mom and Booker being a couple, and it was no problem for Chip now that he knew they wouldn't have to move to Atlanta. The thing he wasn't clear about was how Booker could live in their house. They didn't have any wheelchair ramps. So would they have to move anyway? Mom had once told him that it wouldn't make sense for them to move now that the farm was paid for. So maybe he didn't need to worry about that.

But he couldn't help worrying about how Luther was going to react. Maybe he was still sleeping and didn't know yet. Or maybe he did, and he was so angry he would never speak to Chip again.

Chip had been sitting there five minutes or so, thinking about how quickly things can happen that turn your entire life upside down, when he heard a creaking sound. Someone was coming down the ladder from the barn loft.

Luther walked over and sat down in the shade next to him. "I thought you'd show up here," he said. "What took you so long?"

"I slept in," Chip said.

"Oh."

"Guess you heard the news." Chip looked across the strip of bulldozed earth to the bramble patch and beyond it to the Jungle.

"Booker told me this morning."

"What do you think?"

Luther shrugged. "What do *you* think?"

"About what?" Chip understood Luther's question, but he was afraid any answer he gave might set Luther off.

"About them getting married."

"I guess that would make Booker my stepfather." Chip chose his words carefully. "But he wouldn't really be my father. He'd be, well, just a friend. Same as always." Chip hoped that calling Booker a friend would be okay with Luther—better, anyway, than calling him Dad.

"You heard about the new job?" Luther asked.

"Yeah. Bet Brad's glad about that. They say the old coach was tough as nails."

"Doesn't matter to me," Luther said. "I'm not going out for baseball anyway."

"Me either," Chip said. "I'm going to play soccer."

Luther's head whipped around. Chip didn't know who was more surprised, him or Luther. Chip hadn't known for sure that he was going to go out for soccer instead of baseball until he said it out loud. A big smile spread across Luther's face. "So we'll have Lily ragging on us. She's *twice* as tough as nails."

"Yeah." Chip gave him a big grin. "You want to walk back to the Jungle?"

"Sure," Luther said. "I would've gone earlier, but I was waiting for you."

The swampy pond was still except for the movement of insects over the surface and the occasional splash of a turtle diving in to grab a minnow. The big birds weren't there, and the smaller birds, usually twittering in the trees, were quiet.

"Place feels abandoned," Luther said.

"It is abandoned," Chip replied. "I didn't even see any rabbits this morning."

"They're around. I fed them earlier. Eight, same as yesterday morning." Luther said. "Including Miz Rabbit."

"Guess we got the panthers moved just in time," Chip said. "If there are a few rabbits left, there'll soon be more." He paused. "Wonder how they're doing?"

Chip knew that Luther knew he meant the panthers. He flung himself down on the grass and propped his chin in his hands. "Jumper said that place we let them go is private property, no hunting allowed. And the Panther Reserve is right next to it, in case they want to go there. He said they wouldn't go hungry."

"I guess not," Chip said. "It's just that one morning they were here, having breakfast with their mama, and by dark they were in a totally strange place. It's got to be scary for them."

"That's how I feel," Luther said. "Like one morning I'll be having breakfast in my grandma's kitchen, and by suppertime I'll be sitting at the table in a strange apartment."

"That could happen to me too," Chip said. "Did Booker say anything about where he and Mom plan to live?"

"Not really," Luther replied. "But I did hear Mama tell him there's an apartment available in Mr. Jackson's building."

Alarm bells went off in Chip's head. It was one thing to tell Luther that living in town wouldn't be so bad, but it was something else to think about his own family living there. It would mean having to get rid of *all* their animals!

"What did Booker say?" Chip asked.

"He said he had some other irons in the fire. Whatever that means."

For several minutes neither of them said anything. Then Chip asked, "If you ran away, where would you run to?"

Luther looked out across the pond to the big trees with moss hanging from their branches. "Here."

"Or how about to Jumper's house?" Chip asked. "Reckon they'd take us in?"

Luther almost smiled. "Now there's an idea!"

They fell silent again, because both of them knew their ideas were just fantasies. There was no way to make them happen. Even Lily couldn't negotiate something like—

Suddenly an idea flashed in Chip's mind, so brilliant that he blinked a few times before he could see it clearly enough to put it into words.

"Luther," he exclaimed. "You could negotiate!"

"Negotiate what?"

"Where you live!" Chip yelled. "Instead of just getting mad at your mom, you could *negotiate* with her!"

Luther looked interested, but bewildered. "How?"

"Think of something your mom wants, and trade her that for what *you* want."

Luther shrugged. "Like what? She wants me to make good grades, but I already do that."

"And she wants you to be happy about the wedding!"

"Yeah, so? What do I do? Fake it?"

"So how come you're *not* happy about it?" Not bothering to wait for Luther to answer, Chip shouted, "Because you're going to have to move to town, right? Tell her you'll be happy about the wedding if she'll let you go on living with your grandparents!"

Luther's mouth opened, then closed. It was a minute before he spoke. "What if Grandma and Grandpa don't want me staying with them?"

That was something Chip hadn't considered. But there was no way the Wilsons would want Luther to move away. He always helped his grandfather with the goats and his grandmother with her gardening. Luther was a big help to them. "Remember that day your grandma hurt her leg?" he asked.

"Yeah. What about it?"

"Your mom said maybe it was time your grandparents moved to town because the farm's getting to be too much for them."

"They don't want to move," Luther snapped.

"I know! And if they had you staying with them, maybe they wouldn't have to!"

Luther's dark brown eyes flashed. It was like a light had just gone off in *his* head. He jumped to his feet and socked his fist into the air. "Yes!" he shouted. "That's what I'll do. I'll *negotiate!*"

Then, like a turtle that had just spotted something interesting in the water, Luther dove into the pond, clothes and all.

Laughing, Chip dove in after him. The pond was too shallow for swimming, but the cool water felt great. Chip flipped over on his back and floated, looking up at the sky and the treetops. A shadow passed overhead, and the anhinga landed on a dead branch overlooking the pond. It spread its splendid wings and surveyed its territory.

Chip thought about what Jumper had said: *It's going to be your job to protect these last wild places.*

30
The Wedding Goat

Justin was already at the Wilson house when Chip got there, helping Brad get his sound system ready to play wedding music. Leaving his good clothes in Luther's room, Chip hurried out to help set up folding chairs on the lawn. Then he and Luther helped Mr. Wilson put a long table in the shade of the big camphor tree. Mrs. Wilson decorated the table with flowers, leaving space in the middle for the wedding cake.

A woman Chip had never seen before was helping prepare the food in the kitchen. Mrs. Wilson kept running back and forth between the house and the outdoor setup. She moved a few of the chairs around, arranging them just so, and tied big ribbons on the aisle seats. When she was satisfied with the way everything looked, she called to Mr. Wilson, Luther, and Chip, "You all go get dressed now. Booker will be bringing Kate and the two brides over soon."

Chip and Luther had just finished getting dressed when the front door banged open and the lady who'd been helping in the kitchen called out in a Spanish accent, "Why, Lee-lee! You are so beautiful!"

Chip looked down the hall. The lady from the kitchen, who now had on a turquoise dress and looked pretty beautiful herself, was standing in front of a small person who looked a lot like Lily—except that she was wearing a frilly white dress.

"Luther," Chip hissed. "Come here. *This* you are not going to believe!"

"You're right," Luther exclaimed as he came into the hall. "I don't believe it!"

"Oh look!" Chip called out. "It's Lily, modeling the junior high soccer team's new uniform."

"Or else she's practicing to be homecoming queen," Luther snickered.

Lily folded her arms and gazed at them with amused contempt. "Why would I want to be a homecoming queen when I can be the school's star soccer player?"

"Not in that getup," Chip informed her.

"I know," Lily sighed. "My mother's small, but she's a tough negotiator, and she drives a *very* hard bargain. Not only do I have to wear a dress, I have to be *in* the wedding."

"In exchange for what?" Chip asked.

Lily smiled, and when she did, she looked like the real Lily. "That lady," she said, jabbing her thumb in the direction of the kitchen, where the pretty woman in the turquoise dress had gone. "She's Miguel's mother."

"Really?"

"The only way she and Miguel could stay in the country was if somebody sponsored them, like, you know, helped them find a place to live and a job and stuff. My mother's health isn't so good right now, and my dad's been talking about hiring somebody to help her in the house. I said why not Miguel's mom? That way they could live here and Miguel could go to our school next year. With him, my soccer team will be *totally* unbeatable."

219

"Are you going to have to wear dresses from now on?" Chip asked.

"Are you kidding?" Lily laughed. "I'm a better negotiator than that!"

Chip looked at Luther and grinned. "You're a pretty good negotiator too, Luther."

"I guess." Luther sounded pleased at the compliment. "I wish I could've convinced Mama to let me live here all the time. But getting to stay with Grandma and Grandpa through the summer and spend weekends here after school starts next fall is pretty good, isn't it?"

"Sure," Chip agreed. "Especially since the other four days we'll be staying after school to practice soccer anyway."

"Five," Lily said.

"Four!" Luther and Chip yelled.

Lily started to argue, but just then she noticed Miguel standing out on the porch. She banged out the door to talk to him.

"You know, Lily's right," Luther said. "With Miguel, it's going to be an awesome team."

"Yeah!" Chip followed Luther out to the porch to say hi to Miguel.

Within five minutes Booker drove up with Mom, Ruby, and Kate, plus somebody Chip later found out was Booker's best man. Behind them came a car with Richard Jackson, his parents, and his best man, who had flown in from Chicago. Bringing up the rear was a white pickup truck.

"It's Jumper!" Chip yelled joyfully.

"Grandma! Grandpa!" Luther called through the front door. "Mr. and Mrs. Jumper are here!"

More people arrived after that, mostly the Wilsons' friends, a couple of Mom's friends, and a few of Mr. Jackson's friends from school, including Mr. O'Dell. With guests arriving and introductions being made and cameras clicking, Chip never noticed when the wedding cake got moved out to the long table. At some point he looked over and there it was, tall and white and beautiful, surrounded by spectacular flower arrangements.

Eventually all the guests were seated. Booker and Richard and their best men waited up front with the preacher, while the rest of the wedding party stood on the porch until it was time to march. The marching part reminded Chip a little bit of a Pet Parade he and Luther and Lily had been in once, with music playing and somebody telling you when it was your turn to go and reminding you to leave space between yourself and whoever is walking ahead of you.

Kate, who was maid of honor for both Mom and Ruby, went first. Chip and Luther came next, each carrying a wedding ring. Then came Lily, carrying flowers. The brides came down the ramp last. Mr. Wilson took Ruby's arm and walked with her, and Justin escorted Mom down the aisle.

The ceremony was short. Before Chip knew it, they were at the "I do" part. At the signal, he and Luther stepped forward—Luther to give Richard a ring for Ruby, and Chip to give Booker a ring to put on Mom's finger. At the end, the two couples turned around to face their guests. Lily handed Ruby and Mom each a bouquet of roses, which the brides were supposed to toss out into the crowd. Kate had told Chip that according to tradition, whoever caught the bride's bouquet would be the next one to get married.

Mom immediately flung her bouquet off to the left. Miguel's mom, leaping high like a baseball fielder, caught it. Then Ruby raised her bouquet to fling it off to the right. But instead of throwing it, she dropped it on the ground and let out the most piercing wail Chip had ever heard.

"Goat, you are going to *die!*" Ruby shrieked, and took off running in the direction of the food table.

Naturally everyone looked that way, including Chip. What he saw was unbelievable, yet at the same time no surprise at all somehow. Old Billy was standing on his hind legs at the table, his front feet on the bottom layer of the wedding cake and his face buried up to his eyeballs in the top layer.

Probably what saved Old Billy's life was that Justin outran Ruby and got there first. He jerked Billy's head sideways out of the cake. Unfortunately, the top layer of the cake got knocked off and went sliding onto the grass.

"My beautiful wedding," Ruby moaned. "It's ruined!"

"Not at all," Richard said, running up and putting his arms around her. "It's the bride that counts, and she's still beautiful. Plus intelligent, charming, and—"

"—she loves goats," Booker said, wheeling up.

Ruby gave him a look. "Not *this* goat. I should take a shotgun to him."

"Now, I wouldn't do anything that drastic." Mr. Wilson turned to the wedding guests and called out, "Jumper, did you happen to bring that tranquilizer gun with you?"

"Afraid not." Jumper grinned. "I wasn't expecting wildlife at a wedding."

During all of this, Billy, who had icing from beard to horns, glared at the people around him and kept right on chewing.

Mom laughed and pointed at Mr. Wilson. "It's your fault, Sam. All these years you've been bringing brides for Old Billy and never once gave him a wedding party. I guess he figured this should be *his* wedding."

"Poor Billy," Booker laughed. "A wedding at last and no bride."

"He doesn't care if there's a bride or not," Ruby grumbled. "All he wants is *cake.*"

Justin took Billy back to the pasture while Chip and Luther did their best to clean up the mess. Mr. Wilson told them to put the destroyed cake in a bucket and take it to Billy, since it was fairly certain that nobody else would want to eat cake cleaned up off the ground.

Ruby had Kate bring out some of their gourmet hand-dipped chocolates to serve the guests in place of cake. "I don't mind people remembering this as the chocolate wedding," Ruby said. "I just don't want them remembering it as the goat wedding."

Chip and Luther finished the cleanup, then went to the bathroom to wash the icing off their hands and clothes. When they came back out onto the front porch, people were standing in the shade drinking punch or sitting in chairs with plates of food, talking and laughing.

Booker rolled his wheelchair up the ramp onto the porch and called in a voice that boomed across the yard, "Friends, family, kids, and stray goats, your attention, please! I have an announcement."

Everybody stopped talking to listen, the way Chip imagined all the ballplayers on Booker's team did when he called them to attention.

"A couple of weeks ago," Booker said, "there was a guy trying to build a meatpacking plant in our neighborhood, over at what we call the Old Place. You folks who live around here know what I'm talking about, or maybe you read about it in the paper."

Chip could see people looking puzzled. He was puzzled himself, wondering why Booker would want to bring that up at his wedding. But Mom, who was standing behind Booker with her hands on the back of his wheelchair, was smiling. She seemed to know what was coming.

Booker kept talking. "Back when my mama was a girl, she

knew the owner, Mrs. Franklin. After the Franklins' house burned down and they moved to Atlanta, she and Mama used to trade Christmas cards. That was a long time ago, but when I asked at the place where Mrs. Franklin used to live, I found out what nursing home she's in now. I went to see her, and we had a real nice visit."

It was becoming clear, at least to Chip, that Booker was building up to something. Everyone stayed quiet, not even chewing, to be sure they didn't miss what he was going to say next.

"To make a long story short, she sold me that Old Place. It now belongs to me and this lady in blue." Booker reached up and caught hold of one of Mom's hands.

Chip shot a quick glance at Mom. Her blue eyes sparkled and her cheeks were rosy pink. She looked happier than Chip could ever remember seeing her in his whole life.

There was a smatter of applause. When it quieted down, Mr. Wilson called out, "That Old Place will make a mighty fine farm!"

"Afraid not," Booker said. "Mrs. Franklin is nobody's fool. After I told her what that Blake fellow was trying to do, she brought in a lawyer and canceled Blake's lease. She decided to sell the property to Betty and me. But first she had papers drawn up stating that the back half with the trees and the pond can never be farmed. I had to sign on the dotted line, promising to leave that land in native vegetation, just like it is now."

From out on the lawn came a loud "Wonderful!" It was Mr. O'Dell. "A wild place where wild things can live in peace!"

Chip, who was standing on the porch between Luther and Kate, stepped closer to Booker's wheelchair and asked, "But where are *we* going to live?"

It was Mom who answered. "For the time being, right where we're living now," she said. "But I'm putting our place up for sale. Being on the highway, it's zoned commercial, so we should get a good price for it. Enough to build us a new house on the Old Place. One with wide doors and ramps and all, to make it easier for Booker to get around."

"Oh, Mom!" Kate shrieked. "That will be *awesome.*"

"Yeah!" Chip said, looking over at Luther. Luther's grin was about a mile wide.

Booker squeezed Mom's hand. "You know, Betty, I never had any kids of my own. But if you want my opinion, I think they're smarter than goats. And have much better manners." He gave Chip a wink. "Even the hungriest boy I know wouldn't stick his face in a wedding cake before the guests got served."

Acknowledgments

I would like to thank the following:

• My student specialist, Torey McCluskey, and his mother Wendy for their help with details related to "how things are" in schools (at least, some schools) in Florida.

• Tracy Wilson, a professional wildlife rehabber, who rescues wildcats in the U.S. and Ecuador, for her valuable advice on what's involved in tranquilizing a wildcat.

• Dr. Christopher Sinigalliano of the Southeast Environmental Research Program of Florida International University for the information he provided about the Everglades, including Seminole culture and panther conservation, and for his and his wife Marybeth's contributions to protecting the Florida Everglades and wildcats there and elsewhere.

For information about Florida panthers, you can check out these links:

http://www.panther.state.fl.us/
http://www.nwf.org/floridapanther/
http://www.panthersociety.org/faq.html
http://www.eparks.org/wildlife_protection/wildlife_facts/
    florida_panther.asp

ROSA JORDAN is an environmental activist, a member of Earthways Foundation's board of directors, and author of LOST GOAT LANE, THE GOATNAPPERS, CYCLING CUBA, and DANGEROUS PLACES: TRAVELS ON THE EDGE. She lives with her husband Derek in the Monashee Mountains of British Columbia.

FULTON